BOY CRAZY

1960-1962

The High School Diary

Angela Weiss

I do not assume that woman is better than man.
I do assume she has a different way of looking at things.
Susan B. Anthony

BOY CRAZY 1960-1962: THE HIGH SCHOOL DIARY

Bearissa Books, Los Angeles, California

Because of the dynamic nature of the Internet, addresses and links may have changed since publication and may no longer be valid.

www.boycrazybook.com
boycrazybook@yahoo.com
https://www.facebook.com/boycrazybook
https://twitter.com/boycrazybook

Cover design: Angela Weiss with assistance from Kevin Canes

ISBN: (sc) 978-0-692-97433-9
ISBN: (e) 978-0-692-97449-0

DEDICATION

This book is dedicated to the wonderful readers of *Boy Crazy: The Secret Life of a 1950s Girl* whose appreciation of that diary novel caused this sequel to be published and to my generous Albany friends, especially Eva, Ric, Alice, Tony V, Doreen, and Yeats.

IN MEMORIAM

Kind, talented engineer-physicist-author (*Radar Man*) Edward Lovick, Jr. (1919-2017)

Generous, brilliant rabbi-therapist-author (*The Poisoned Crop*) Ephraim Rubinger (1944-2018)

CONTENTS

INTRODUCTION

Presuming that you have read *Boy Crazy: The Secret Life of a 1950s Girl,* this sequel refers to events and characters in that book without repeating details. The end lists can help refresh your memory.

As Sergeant Joe Friday said on the 1960s TV program, *Dragnet*, "Names have been changed to protect the innocent."

It was 1960 in Albany, NY. I was still boy crazy and the world continued to be crazy!

DIARY EXCERPTS

1960 Albany High School (AHS) Sophomore

Happy families are all alike; each unhappy family is unhappy in its own way.

Anna Karenina **by Tolstoy**

Tuesday, February 16, 1960: Family Matters

Setting my hair, I sat at my cherished white dressing table, a 1930s hand-me-down from Sara. As I drifted into a reverie, my full-length mirror image seemed to shift to Sara, abruptly departing last August after an attempted rape, and then to Grandma, arriving in September. She had fluid in the lungs and high blood pressure after a stroke a few years ago. Mom's two brothers didn't take in Grandma, who asked Mom to stay home with her. Is Mom feeling guilty because she couldn't quit her job? Grandma should have understood that Mom's state typist earnings helped pay the mortgage. And that was before Dad lost his sales job last month after many years at the Surplus Store! This month, he's earned nothing trying to sell vacuum cleaners door-to-door. We're lucky that Mom's bosses are trying to pay her more, but she said, "Don't hold your breath. The bureaucrats may take forever to reclassify my job at a higher grade."

Wednesday, February 17, 1960: Poor Mom

Since Grandma's funeral Sunday, Mom has seemed like a changed woman. Since December I've been in a cold war with both parents. Religion resulted in their forcing me to turn down my only invitation to the Jack Frost semi-formal dance. Intelligent Craig dances like Fred Astaire but isn't Jewish. Though Mom's not my favorite person, I almost prefer her annoying bossiness and nagging to her new glum preoccupation. Are the pills the doctor brought Saturday, after Mom discovered her mother dead in bed, sedating Mom? At least Dad's worry about Mom has squelched his temper tantrums.

Craig

Thursday, February 18, 1960: Lon

Smart, blond Lon's call was a happy escape from the gloomy home atmosphere. Listening on my white princess extension phone, I sat against the padded, mint green vinyl headboard with my adored green ballerina wallpaper behind me. With my satiny Heywood Wakefield maple desk in view, I answered homework questions from cute Lon, whom I've wanted to date since we became 1958 classmates. Romanticizing Lon's platonic image of me will require a fairy godmother's magic.

Friday, February 19, 1960: Debating

Nice-looking, witty Mr. O opened our AHS debate tournament for twenty NYS schools. I felt proud of our school for helping found, in 1925, the National Forensic League (NFL) with 200,000 current members! The present NFL topic is whether our country should use the Conant Report recommendations to improve American high schools.

I'm elated about winning one of my first three debates. Do sophomores Hank, Neal, and Udeh win most debates because boys are better at debating or because Mr. O has helped them since September? Although one junior girl is on the debate team, I as alternate am the only sophomore girl. Mr. O wears bow ties, calls himself a confirmed bachelor, and seems a bit prissy. I'm fine if he prefers males to females as kids say, but he should coach girls as much as boys.

Still excited about the debate, I had a blast tonight at the Center (JCC: Jewish Community Center)! After ping-pong with Yeats and former flame Artie, I danced and joked around with Yeats, past boyfriend Steve, Marsha's twins, Doreen's crush Neal, and others. With ex-boyfriend Ray and his date, Yeats took me to Joe's Deli on Madison. The boys ordered hot pastrami-on-rye sandwiches. We girls warmed up with French onion soup *au gratin*.

AHS's Ionic columns

Saturday, February 20, 1960: Tumba

Mom's in a bad way when even amusing parakeet Tumba hasn't made her smile lately. His nightly exercise is flying around the dining room. Perching on shoulders and fingers, he talks a blue streak of nonsense and real words. Tumba cracked me up by chirping for the first time, "For crying out loud!" exactly as Dad shouts it during temper tantrums.

Tumba

Sunday, February 21, 1960: Olympics

Hoping that Americans get more medals than the Russians, I'm proud of the US for hosting thirty countries for the Squaw Valley Winter Olympics in California! Hating winter with its bleak, colorless skies, I don't understand people voluntarily spending hours outdoors on snow sports. Progress: female speed skaters are competing for the first time at the Olympics. My favorite event is figure skating, similar to my beloved dancing!

Wednesday, February 24, 1960: Blue Moon

None of the ten percent of AHS kids who are Jewish boys has invited me to the Blue Moon formal this weekend. Imagining what a great time Craig and I could have had, I'm extremely irritated at the parents!

Friday, February 26, 1960: Hockey

I'm excited about the underdog American hockey players defeating Czechoslovakia, Australia, Sweden, West Germany, and Canada! Without losses, they have yet to play the strong Russian team.

Saturday, February 27, 1960: Too Young

At a Sweet Sixteen party at Victor's house, dancing with tall Rex (actor Kirk Douglas' nephew) was exhilarating! When we went bowling, why did I get only 75 after 104 and 80 last Sunday?

Our group tried to get into cool Mike's Log Cabin, a real log cabin outside and inside at 23 North Swan Street, a Negro area. Yeats, my escort most of the evening, said, "I've heard that Mike's has been around for over thirty years. AHS seniors drink and dance to the jukebox." Since no one had proof of being eighteen, the NYS drinking age, Mike's wouldn't admit us.

We ended up at our usual hangout, the always open Boulevard Cafeteria. Holding machine tickets with printed prices, we slid our trays along the metal tube rack at the food station. I got my favorites: French fries and chocolate milk. Our tickets got punched with bargain prices. Gazing at the Boulevard's tall windows with rounded tops, I was too chicken to ask Yeats whether AHS kids started coming here so boys could sneak peeks at the nudes in the curved ceiling murals. Without waiters to tip, we kids sat talking for ages at long tables coming out from wood-paneled walls before paying the cashier. Mesmerized by Yeats' green eyes, I enjoyed his goodnight kiss.

Yeats

Boulevard Cafeteria (photo from AllOverAlbany.com)

Sunday, February 28, 1960: Medals

I'm overjoyed that these Americans gave the US the most Olympic figure skating medals: David Jenkins, men's gold; the Ludingtons, pairs' bronze; beautiful Carol Heiss from NYC, ladies' gold; and Barbara Roles, ladies' bronze!

Monday, February 29, 1960: Gold and Leap Year

Everyone is thrilled about American hockey players winning all seven games and, on the final Olympics day, their first ever gold medal!

On leap year day, I'm too young to propose. In 1968, I'll be twenty-three, a good age to propose if I'm in love!

Tuesday, March 1, 1960: Mean

After our AHS basketball game against Schuyler, I had fun kidding around with Eva, Xavier, and my ex-boyfriend Paul. Though AHS won 84-42, we couldn't gloat about beating a much smaller school. In the girls' bathroom, Eva smiled and looked pleased after I said, "I'm glad that you've been dating. Every time we meet, you look prettier!"

"Thanks for the encouragement! Xavier and Ric have been avoiding me as if I have the bubonic plague."

"I'm sorry! Since you've had a soft spot for Ric, it must hurt."

"I've felt a bit isolated because they're among the few brainy Schuyler guys. Even though handsome Ric hasn't been romantic as I'd prefer, he was friendly and fun."

"I wonder why they've acted so mean."

"Xavier tends to lead. Who knows what bee is in his bonnet?"

I chuckled. "I'm picturing Xavier in a pink baby bonnet... What else is new?"

"Our girls' homeroom is collecting used toys for Trinity Institution and Giffen Elementary School to win the Red Cross competition. Underprivileged kids without toys can borrow and return them at the library."

"That's a great idea."

Tonight, I thanked God for my memory. I recall conversations long enough to write them in this diary. Taking tests, I picture sentences on pages I've studied.

Schuyler High School geometry class second row left to right: unknown blonde, Eva, & Xavier; third row left to right: Alice (Hackett Junior High classmate) & Ric

Thursday, March 3, 1960: Storm

I hoped that winter's worst was past until this Northeastern blizzard with chilling winds arrived. After Aunt Lila called from NYC, Mom said, "Central Park got over fourteen inches of snow!" Poor Dad! After dropping Mom at work, he's outside every day knocking on doors as a salesman.

Hearing a hit on the radio from a movie I liked, *Theme from A Summer Place*, I imagined romantic beach scenes with cute actor Troy Donahue.

Saturday, March 5, 1960: Carnival

Yeats took me by cab to the Center Purim Carnival. After the basketball game, the best booth we visited was the romantic mock wedding chapel, where we got married! Though I wedded Tad in 1950, marrying Yeats was too much fun to let bigamy stop me! After Yeats and I sat for an abstract portrait, he won the grand prize, a camera! I enjoyed his arm around me and our dances. We talked to many kids, including one of my crushes: amusing Hank. At the Moon (restaurant), we sat with two couples. Spumoni ice cream with green, pink, and chocolate layers was delicious! Yeats' goodnight kisses ended a fabulous evening!

Thursday, March 10, 1960: Dad

After Dad's birthday dinner with cake and candles, Eva's and Doreen's strategy got me around the parents' gentile-dating ban: I met Protestant Craig at the upbeat AHS band concert! After enjoying his arm around me, I walked out on his arm. We both preferred Tchaikovsky's *Marche Slav* to Leroy Anderson's *The Girl I Left Behind*. Liking vocal music the best, I enjoyed the choir singing Vincent Youmans' *Fantasy* with the band. What a terrif evening! Did the birthday tie I gave Dad prevent complaints about driving Craig, as well as Jewish Doreen and Neal, home?

Doreen

Saturday, March 12, 1960: Party

After a fun Craig phone call, Yeats took me to a party whose atmosphere, music, and food were good. With his arm around me all evening, Yeats kissed me a few times. At my house, we thawed out from the freezing temperature by talking and kissing while favorites like *Jamaican Farewell, Day-O,* and *Man Smart Woman Smarter* played on our Harry Belafonte *Calypso* album.

Sunday, March 13, 1960: Music

Dominic's and Zeke's classical music piano recital was impressive! Dominic's Chopin *Polonaise* was my favorite piece.

When cute Lon called, I was disappointed as usual to be asked only about homework.

Dominic

Saturday, March 19, 1960: Beats

Wearing all black (jeans, turtleneck, and beret), Yeats escorted me to the Beatnik Blast at the Center. Wearing white lipstick, heavy black eyeliner, black slacks, and a black turtleneck was fun. Every time we used beat words like *cool*, we got silly and laughed. I danced with Yeats and others. Yeats had his arm around me, held my hand, and danced close, which I adore! After pizza at the Moon, we kissed goodnight a few times, an ideal end to a fun evening!

Sunday, March 20, 1960: Letter

At the kitchen phone desk, I stopped in shock. An envelope with Sara's NYC return address and a recent postmark date was sticking up from a bunch of papers! For seven months I've missed my favorite aunt. News about her is precious. Since the possibility of Mom's snooping in my diary fills me with dread, I followed the golden rule and avoided looking in the envelope. Fear of Mom's reaction prevented my asking what Sara wrote. I've been ashamed to confide in friends about my lack of supportive words after Sara's attack.

Sara playing the piano at age 28 in 1945

Thursday, March 24, 1960: Wanted

The parents have yet to mention Sara's mysterious envelope, which has been on my mind. Something, maybe last night's dream about Sara, made me open my baby book, untouched for years. I've wondered whether the light blue cover meant the parents wanted a boy. Inside was Sara's sweet January 1945 letter, which I had completely forgotten:

Dear Fern,

You can't imagine how thrilled we were when we called the hospital Sunday morning and they told us you had given birth to a baby girl. I didn't want to say anything, but my secret desire was for a girl. I hope that by now you are feeling well and that you've already seen the baby. We wanted to see you Sunday but the hospital said we couldn't come yet. I called Mama and told her the news. She was so thrilled she could hardly talk. She said she was going to call everyone in Gloversville and tell them the good news. I'm anxious to see the baby. I'll see you Thursday evening. Which name have you chosen? I like Angie. Take care of yourself and I'll see you soon.

Love, Sara

P.S. How is the proud Papa doing? Did he get enough cigars to hand out?

Though pleased that Sara wanted a girl, influenced my name, and loved me from the start, I'm sad about losing her suddenly last summer. Being unable to see her in NYC is frustrating.

Saturday, March 26, 1960: Contest

On the train to NYC for the Baird Memorial Latin contest, mother hen Mrs. G said to us six students: "About 250 high schools in eight states are sending 1,000 Latin pupils. This is only the second year AHS has been honored with an invitation. Are you ready to sight read and translate Latin prose?"

When senior heartthrob Parker answered by quoting Julius Caesar, "*Veni, vidi, vici!*" (I came, I saw, I conquered), we cracked up. Before and after the contest at NY University, I had fun with Parker, my ex Steve, and a junior class BMOC (big man on campus). At Radio City Music Hall, *Home from the Hill*, a drama about a powerful Texas family, was absorbing. I like actor George Hamilton who played the son.

Returning home, I imagined Sara playing Ludwig, her ebony baby grand piano, only twenty-three blocks from Radio City. I could almost hear her voice, husky from smoking, describe 160 West 73rd Street, as I helped her pack to move to Albany in 1958:

> In 1929, this musicians' building was specially constructed with heavy duty hardwood floors to support grand pianos. A rubber layer underneath the floor, double walls, and heavy doors provide soundproofing, as do the layouts: pantries, bathrooms, and hallways are barriers between living rooms and neighboring apartments.

Tuesday, March 29, 1960: Craig

When Craig called Sunday, I said, "Mr. Astaire, you would have loved the Rockettes' stage show. I missed you in NYC."

"Ginger, a vision of the Rockettes will motivate me to excel in Latin so I can go next year!" he quipped.

After calling Monday, today Craig accompanied me to Doreen's house for ping-pong with her and JP. We got really silly, batting the ball on the walls and ceiling and laughing hysterically. Craig carried my books home. I had a blast because of his great sense of humor!

Friday, April 1, 1960: Tempted

Craig's dance party had the best guests, including fascinating Dominic and mysterious Zeke, who intrigues me. I enjoyed the April Fools' jokes of a miniature Craig, his ten-year-old brother. Intelligent conversation and exceptional personalities made it one of the best parties ever.

Chatting and laughing with Eva whom I miss this year, I asked, "Does my charming ex have the same Schuyler girlfriend?"

"The gossip is that Paul also has Catholic school girlfriends. He looks a bit down lately."

"I volunteer to console him." We giggled. "Eva, are you busy with school play rehearsals?"

She grinned. "Memorizing lines keeps me out of mischief."

Romantic Zeke put his arm around me; whispered wonderful, deep (at least they seemed that way at the time), serious things in my ear; ran his piano fingers through my hair; played with my fingers; and helped me on with my coat. After sitting on his lap in the car going home, I found his goodnight kiss heavenly! Zeke tempted me to let myself be carried away. Fortunately, parent chaperones kept things from getting out of control.

Saturday, April 2, 1960: Mail

I'm intercepting Saturday's mail. Sara's envelope must have arrived then for me to have missed it after school. I dreamt about her using a favorite word to praise someone: *haimish*, which she defined as warm and unpretentious. "The Yiddish means homey or cozy," she explained.

Friday, April 8, 1960: Addressee

With the parents at synagogue services, I had a brainstorm: it's not snooping if I'm included in the address. Praying to God and holding my breath like dynamite about to explode, I found Sara's envelope in the same place. *The Weisses* on the envelope made me sigh with relief. Finding nothing inside, I felt let down. Under my frilly headboard light, I read Leon Uris's stirring novel *Exodus*. I'm in love with hero Ari Ben Canaan.

Saturday, April 9, 1960: Suddenly

Yeats and I saw *Suddenly, Last Summer,* starring Elizabeth Taylor, Katharine Hepburn, and Montgomery Clift. Trying to figure out this psychological mystery based on Tennessee Williams' play, I was fascinated but confused.

At Joe's Deli, we ran into Doreen and JP. In the ladies' room when Doreen requested an update, I said, "Last Saturday with Yeats was fun. After dancing and ping-pong at the Center, we talked at the Boulevard. At my house, we danced to Johnny Mathis romantic songs, like *The Twelfth of Never*,

When I Am with You, Wild Is the Wind, and *Come to Me,* until he left at 1:30 AM after kissing me goodnight."

"Are you in love?"

I giggled. "I love all interesting boys, including Yeats, Luke, Craig, and Dominic. Thanks again for your great idea of enjoying gentiles at school events and on the phone. How are you and JP doing?"

"Since JP spotted me in German class, which has more boys than girls, he's been asking me out. I like him and have fun on our dates."

The delightful date ended with Yeats taking me home in a taxi and kissing me goodnight thrice.

Tuesday, April 12, 1960: *Exodus*

I've learned so much from this touching historical novel about the brave people who fought to create Israel for Holocaust survivors and other Jews. Did the book, which has deeply affected me, cause last night's recurring nightmare? At the beach, a gigantic tidal wave as tall as a skyscraper was about to break near the shore. I ran for my life up the beach. Looking over my shoulder, I saw the wave gaining on me. With escape impossible as the water was about to drown me, I woke myself up. The dream was scary, like Holocaust survivors' lives. I've been tearful about countries refusing to admit them after all they went through to survive during World War II.

Thursday, April 14, 1960: Hot

With the high over eighty degrees, I skipped down the street buoyed by spring fever! The newspaper lists fifty-seven as today's normal high.

Saturday, April 16, 1960: Easter

I was happy to accept Dominic's invitation to services tonight at his Greek Orthodox Church downtown on Lancaster Street. During melodic chanting, I admired the stained glass windows, velvet drapes, pastel flowers painted on gold-trimmed walls, colorful murals, priest's and assistant's embroidered white robes, priest's high rounded crown, and ornate gold and silver religious objects! Though Jesus isn't my god and the service was in Greek, the ritual was so beautiful and moving that a tear rolled down my cheek. Dominic's tall outgoing brunette mom and shorter bald jovial dad were fun!

Sunday, April 17, 1960: Lydia

On a spring-like Easter, we drove to Gloversville. On a walk without parents, Cousin Lydia shared eighth-grade experiences: "My father and your mother attended Estee Junior High centuries ago! Can you believe that I have my father's 1916 Latin teacher who must be at least seventy? She props her skinny, arthritic leg on the open drawer of her desk and has trouble moving around and writing on the blackboard."

I replied, "All Latin teachers must be old. At Hackett, white-haired Miss W was in the hospital for ages. This year, gray-haired but peppy Mrs. G has taken us to contests.

You're lucky that Gloversville starts Latin in seventh grade. You and I are both in second-year Latin. Do you like Cicero?"

"It's better than Caesar's boring war stories."

"How's your boyfriend?"

"Even though he's five inches shorter, Len is smart and keeps me laughing during long phone talks. He has no accent though he came from Europe at age four. His parents are Holocaust survivors."

"Does he still try to make out at parties?"

"Yes! During Spin the Bottle in his basement, we go into the laundry room to kiss. He tries to keep me there with long French kisses. His octopus hands try to go everywhere, especially my big boobs."

"That sounds annoying! My mother mentioned kissing games at Roaring Twenties Gloversville teen parties. I wonder whether Mom's crush, cousin Sam Berger, tried to touch her boobs." We girls chuckled.

My eyes widened in surprise as Lydia said, "Sam was a diplomat in London, Tokyo, and New Zealand's capital, Wellington."

Ella added, "The last we heard, he's in Athens, Greece."

Lydia got back to Len. "How can a thirteen-year-old expect sex?"

"At fourteen, Myles was greedy for experience with as many girls as possible, despite his friend saying that Myles was *going with* me. Rather than be one of many girls a boy uses, I want to feel loved by a boyfriend who's interested in only me."

I nodded agreement when Lydia predicted, "If Len had his way, after his conquest he'd probably date someone new."

<u>Monday, April 18, 1960: Girl Talk</u>

I love Easter vacation: no homework and nice weather!

Eva called to share, "I heard that Xavier, who still has a crush on you, gets people who drive to take him past your house."

"I'm astonished. He last called six months ago when we double-dated at the movies. What's new?"

"I'm friendlier with the less intellectual, wilder crowd. A tall guy named Gordon has been fun at the movies. What's happening with you?"

"Thanks again for helping me get around my parents! I'm enjoying Craig's company often. The night meeting of the four AHS literary societies was a great opportunity to see him. The next Saturday, after being together at the local Shaker High Latin contest, he helped me choose a raincoat downtown and treated me to a sundae. Unlike most boys, he has good taste and the patience to shop. Holding hands helped make it a wonderful day! He and Dominic have called a couple of times a week. Easter services with Dominic's family felt like seeing a majestic pageant in a movie."

"How about Casanova?"

"Because debonair Zeke's hard to resist, I'm safer if my good-girl reputation prevents dates. Dominic invited me to their joint piano recital...Can you join Craig, Neal, Marsha, Marie, and me for tennis and bowling Wednesday?"

"Thanks, but play rehearsals are daily. Besides, I'm the world's klutziest athlete." We chuckled.

At the bowling alley, I got 93 and 100 and talked to smart Hank, who's Jewish. I wish he'd ask me out.

Tuesday, April 19, 1960: Who's Better?

After Craig and Yeats called, I played tennis and bowled my high of 118!

Yeats took me to the Center where I had a blast dancing with him and others. At ping-pong, he wins about half the time. I said flirtatiously, "Yeats, you're nicer than other boys because you let me win some games."

He laughed. "I don't let you win. You're too good to beat all the time."

"It doesn't seem to bother you."

"Why should it? Ping-pong doesn't take strength like football. Why shouldn't girls be as good?"

I smiled mischievously. "Do you think that boys are smarter than girls?"

He chuckled. "We're smart enough to avoid that question!" I giggled. After fun at the Moon, I enjoyed his goodnight kisses.

Thursday, April 21, 1960: Pajama Party

Vacation continues to be perfect! The Tennessee Williams movie *The Fugitive Kind* with Marlon Brando, Joanne Woodward, and Anna Magnani was interesting. Though set in the South, it's supposed to be based on a Greek tragedy, *Orpheus Descending.*

In the evening at Doreen's, she, JP, Yeats, and I danced and enjoyed doubles ping-pong. After the boys left, Doreen said, "Yeats seems very nice. It's fun to double with two juniors."

I agreed. "How are things with JP?"

"I like him but feel too young for a steady boyfriend, not that he has asked." We giggled. "We have a good time, but know each other only casually. I'm shy and he avoids serious talk like most boys."

"I know what you mean. The boys I'm comfortable talking to beyond a fun level, like Dominic, are forbidden. Do you still go for Neal?"

"Angela, I've given up though I can't help feeling attracted to someone as smart as Neal."

"Brains are one reason I like Yeats." After admiring Doreen's new spring outfits, I stayed over to keep girl-talking until late.

Saturday, April 23, 1960: Find

I've kept my eyes open for the contents of Sara's envelope while stopping short of opening parents' drawers. I'd feel too guilty. While they played cards at the Levines' house, I noticed that the envelope was gone. Since we all use the phone desk, looking through those papers didn't seem like snooping. My heart pounded when I spotted Sara's handwriting on a sheet of stationery dated last month. "Thank you, God!" I whispered.

To the therapist of Fern and Herm Weiss:

My sister and I have had such overly strong family ties that we don't give our mates the opportunity to relate to us fully. Her husband and my boyfriend Mort have felt jealous and insecure. My therapist has mandated no contact with my family at least until January 1961, to let both couples strengthen their relationships.

I was shocked to learn that my parents have a therapist. Did they start after Grandma C's death? Did Mom hide Sara's letter to avoid telling me? Putting the letter back exactly where it was, I decided to say nothing.

Is Sara back with Mort despite his jilting her for singer Martha Schlamme? I drifted off to sleep more hopeful about seeing Sara. Without her, I feel trapped and alone with the parents.

Sunday, April 24, 1960: Daylight Savings

Enjoying the longer day, I repeated and memorized my upcoming campaign speech in front of the mirror: "If elected, I will work hard for the benefit of the junior class next year."

Monday, April 25, 1960: Elections

We ten nominees for junior class offices gave our speeches. Ugh! I had to look at my cards when nerves made me go blank as usual.

Thursday, April 28, 1960: Officers

At our excellent school play, *You Can't Take It with You*, by Kaufman and Hart, I was happy to feel Craig's arm around me. We had fun talking to Dominic and Eva!

In the girls' room, I told Eva, "Udeh beat Craig and me for class president. I was for Craig, but Udeh's enthusiastic, rather than jealous or competitive, when good things happen to others. I commiserated with disappointed Craig, who asked, 'Angela, why do you look happier after losing?'" Eva chuckled before I added, "I couldn't reveal that no one invited me to the Patroon prom when I was school president and I'd rather date cute boys than be an officer! The only office a girl won was secretary. I was the only girl up for president. With any chance of winning, I would have declined the nomination as I did at Hackett."

Eva smiled. "Is your least favorite thing on earth, public speaking, getting easier?"

We both giggled when I shook my head no. "Eva, I can't imagine how you remember tons of lines in a play and act in a convincing manner as a particular character without being self-conscious and scared to death."

"It's fun to use my imagination and escape from myself."

Saturday, April 30, 1960: Sadie Hawkins

Yeats and I laughed at the comic movie *Wake Me When It's Over*. After sodas, he took me home and kissed me goodnight. Enjoying his company, I like looking into his beautiful long-lashed eyes while listening to him. In my Sadie Hawkins role, I was glad that he accepted my invitation to the XEA sorority dance!

Monday, May 2, 1960: Cold

Last night, the low was thirty-three degrees. My parents mentioned five inches of May snow the year I was born. In third grade at Mayfield School in Colonie, I recall saying, "This May snow is unfair. On the *House Party* radio show, Art Linkletter mentions sunny Los Angeles winter weather in the seventies! I'd like to be in his *Kids Say the Darndest Things* interviews." I dread May snow and a short summer if snow starts in October!

Thursday, May 5, 1960: Mr. P

Spotting me walking home from school, my fun freshman citizenship education (social studies) teacher Mr. P gave me a lift. Feeling happy to hear about his new baby boy, I said, "Congratulations!"

Friday, May 6, 1960: Gym and Grace

To avoid the *Brain* label, I changed the subject when kids asked about my report card. I felt happy about all *A*s, except a *B* in gym, where we hardly do anything in the ten minutes between changing into and out of our ugly green bloomer uniforms. They flatter only a perfect figure.

Craig called and met me at Schuyler, where we sat together, held hands, and laughed often at the humor of *Our Hearts Were Young and Gay*. After I requested star Eva's autograph, she laughed and signed my program, "To my biggest fan Angela: Love from Grace Kelly."

"Your coloring resembles hers!" I noted.

Eva chuckled and shook her head. "Joke! Joke!"

Eva blushed when I said, "You're better at comedy than Grace. I admire your bravery and ability as a stage actress!"

Craig took me home in a cab. He laughed when I said, "Teaching English and geometry today for Student Government Day confirmed teaching's last place on my career list." What a special evening!

Saturday, May 7, 1960: Handicaps

Yeats drove me northwest of Albany on Route 20 to West-mere for miniature golf. When he won, I said, "I love miniature golf, but need a handicap because you're good at real golf and I have yet to play."

He chuckled. "You can have a golf handicap if I get one when we play tennis."

"But I'm only a beginner at tennis," I objected.

"Then I'll take a ping-pong handicap. You're good at that."

I laughed before replying, "So are you!"

At the Center, I enjoyed dances with Luke and two other agreeable boys and ping-pong with another boy.

Sunday, May 8, 1960: Hellman

After eating out for Mother's Day, we entered the new Hell-man Theatre on Washington Avenue across from Albany State College for Teachers. Dad said, "You can't tell from the plain exterior that a thousand seats are inside!"

Mom said, "I like the patterned carpet and curved, cut-out room divider in this lobby."

I commented, "I like the circular lounge, especially the mural on the curved wall and donut-shaped sofa with the evergreen bush in the center."

Walking down the aisle to our seats, Mom exclaimed, "These gold drapes, gold seats in the center section, and blue seats in the side sections are attractive!" We all laughed at the Doris Day and David Niven family movie *Please Don't Eat the Daisies*. Almost three months after Grandma died, Mom seems more upbeat.

Friday, May 13, 1960: New Idea

After thanking God for getting me through Friday the Thirteenth, I wondered whether the parents started their secret therapy after Sara left. Her note to the therapist suggested that family comedian Dad lost Mom's and my attention for the year Sara lived with us. I cringed recalling Dad's cruelty after Sara's attack. Did Dad's jealous hostility drive charismatic, humorous Sara away? Or am I fooling myself to escape my own guilt?

Saturday, May 14, 1960: Beehive

After a fun half-hour conversation with Dominic, I was happy when a florist delivered Yeats' six gorgeous yellow roses in a wrist corsage for tonight's XEA dance. To divert attention from my ugly old formal, I had my nails polished in gold and my hair teased into the latest beehive style. At the dance at the Hampton Hotel, we sat with Doreen, JP, Marsha, and my 1959 XEA picnic date Phil, who all looked attractive. Marsha, Doreen, and others flattered me: "I love your hair. You look just like pretty Jenny in the Genesee beer TV commercial." At Barone's nightclub, we danced to a quartet and singer. At 3AM, after a fun evening of hand holding and feeling Yeats' arm around me, I enjoyed about six goodnight kisses.

Sunday, May 15, 1960: Music

A Gloversville family picnic in a park was fun! Away from our parents, Lydia asked, "Do you ever hear from our aunt?"

My description of Sara's letter with the contact ban made Lydia roll her eyes about the strange ways of adults. I asked, "When you took piano lessons, did your mother bug Sara to say that you had talent, as my mother did?"

Lydia laughed. "How did you know? Since our mother was also learning piano, she kept trying to get Sara to say that she was a genius, too! We were all mediocre at best!"

Giggling, I said, "Poor Sara! Though she encouraged me, she must have had a hard time keeping a straight face hearing me bang away while my mother said things like, 'Angela must have your musical ability. Doesn't she play with an excellent touch?'"

Ella said, "Wasn't Bach her favorite musician? She admired that he composed counter-melodies in the same piece."

I responded, "That sounds familiar. Did the music start with one melody and have a second melody start a little later with both playing at the same time?"

Lydia replied, "I paid too little attention to get that far. Do you remember the movies she raved about?"

Ella answered, "*Twelve Angry Men* about jurors and *Marty* about the romance of an unmarried man living with his mother. I remember her singing *Somebody Bad Stole de Wedding Bell* and *Everybody Loves Saturday Night* while playing Baby, the red, white, and blue accordion."

Lydia added, "She got excited about a music career after winning a kids' contest while playing the violin."

I responded, "That's news! Does Gloversville still have that contest?"

Lydia shrugged. "It's hard to imagine this one-horse town having such a contest."

Ella said, "It was the Roaring Twenties."

I commented, "I miss her and am grateful that she bought Tumba." At home, Tumba, who clearly favored Sara, included her name in his monologue.

Monday, May 16, 1960: Porch Fun

After walking me home, Craig made me laugh as we sat on our porch and talked about school. He considerately left before my parents got home from work.

Wednesday, May 18, 1960: Prom

Doreen, excited about going to the junior prom with JP, said, "I'm glad it's early enough to buy a dress without rushing. Can you come with my mother and me after school tomorrow?"

"That sounds like fun. I'd love to help!" I'm happy that Doreen, who deserves the best, will attend the prom with someone she likes! If I could date gentiles, one of almost 200 junior boys might ask me if Yeats doesn't. I'll think about something else to avoid a repeat of my eighth-grade prom hurt and disappointment.

Saturday, May 21, 1960: Manly

At Dominic's piano recital, I felt excited watching his manly, strong hands on the keys! While his beautiful classical music enthralled me, I drifted back to Tuesday at school when he said, "I love you." He probably meant it as a friend. It would be nice if he meant it romantically because I like him a lot. What would happen if religion didn't keep us from dating?

Saturday, May 28, 1960: Whirling

At the Temple Israel dance, I felt impatient to dance while standing around chatting with ten boys, including crushes Luke and Hank. The fun started when terrific dancers Rex and Luke whirled me around the floor. I was sad that my parents' curfew forced me to decline Luke's invite to a party afterwards. My consolation will be having Cousin Ron and his parents at our house this holiday weekend! Hal is busy with graduate school.

Saturday, June 5, 1960: Julie Kaiser

At Washington Park, Doreen said, "My parents' friends, who saw Tulip Queen Julie crowned last month, said, 'She has pretty reddish hair like yours. You should run for Queen in three years.' Thanking them, I could hardly keep a straight face." She tittered.

"That's flattering!"

"It's crazy, as if all it takes to be a beauty queen is hair color. In 1963, I hope to be away at college learning to be a teacher," she remarked.

"College away tops a year of smiling and acting charming at Albany public appearances."

Thursday, June 9, 1960: Marathon

I studied for finals, coming too soon, before and after one of my longest phone conversations. Ninety minutes flew by as I listened to thought-provoking, well-read Dominic talk about politics and current events.

Saturday, June 11, 1960: Clue

Having loved Nancy Drew mysteries, like the *The Clue in the Diary* and *The Clue of the Broken Locket*, I wondered whether last night's dream was a clue: I was in Sara's NYC apartment as she looked for an important paper in her desk. In case dreams mean something, while home alone I looked at papers on the phone desk. About to give up, I spied this note among some bills:

> Angela and I should also not correspond until January, so you can tell Angela about all this in whatever way you see fit. Love and Kisses XXXXX Sara

Did this arrive with the letter to my parents' therapist? Sara's thinking of me and sending *Love and Kisses* made me feel better, i.e., less guilty. I resent the parents' hiding this from me!

Tuesday, June 14, 1960: Final Cards

My final report card with *A*s in every subject made me less nervous about upcoming exams. I like the AHS custom of kids signing final report envelopes.

Marsha's comment was funny: "Don't let school interfere with your education."

I felt happy reading favorite teacher Mrs. E's note: "To the sweetest, most gracious-speaking student."

I like Craig's poem: "To the greatest kid I know: to a girl who's very pretty, to a girl who's very smart, to a girl whose wit is funny, to the girl who won my heart (as a friend)." Is the unromantic *friend* for my parents' benefit?

Wednesday, June 15, 1960: Favorite Callers

After my English final, Luke, Craig, and Dominic rewarded me with calls. Sad that Dominic has pneumonia, I giggled when he wisecracked, "I cried today about missing finals."

Thursday, June 16, 1960: *Brain*

I phoned Doreen to say, "I need advice. How can I get boys I like to see me more romantically?"

"Is this because of how they signed your report card envelope?" she inquired.

"You're smart! How did you know?"

"My envelope comments showed what people think of me."

"Were your feelings hurt?"

"I was pleasantly surprised. Which ones bothered you?"

"Pal Neal's 'The best of luck to a good old friend' was okay. But Luke signed only his name. Lon signed 'Hi Pal.' Fun Jake, who's in all my classes, joked about my grades: 'Good luck to a kid in a rut (what a rut!).' The only positive comment was from tall, handsome Lee, the smart Negro boy in Latin class: 'Best of luck to a very sweet girl.' I'd like to date him."

"He has a great smile and body and seems very nice! Did Yeats write anything good after dating you all spring?"

It was hard to stop chortling. "He wrote: 'Good luck on your exams.'"

Doreen laughed. "Keep changing the subject when people ask about grades! I'll try to come up with more ways to remove the *Curse of the Brain*." We chuckled before I thanked her and signed off.

Friday, June 17, 1960: Appreciated

At least some nice girls appreciate me. A vivacious, smart blonde in my literary society penned: "Good luck to the most modest girl I know (about marks). Hope you do as well on finals as you did on the midyears. Love n' stuff, Betty."

Our upstairs neighbor's comment made me feel good: "Best of luck always to a very sweet kid. With your smile, *You'll Never Walk Alone.*"

A zany amusing girl wrote: "To *Brain Girl* and the nicest one I know!"

Tall, smart, kind Cara, whose glasses and size have kept her from dating, wrote: "To a sweet, beautiful, charming friend who has been a good sport through times when jokes were made about your marks. I will remember you as valedictorian of AHS."

Cara

Saturday, June 18, 1960: Talk

While studying for finals, I was thankful to hear that Dominic is recovering from scary pneumonia. During two hours of stimulating conversation, he said, "The popular novel *Advise and Consent* keeps my mind occupied while I recuperate. I can't wait to be done with eight dull Eisenhower years after elections this fall!" and "We have permanent egg on our faces after our spy plane was shot down last month by the Russians!" Amused, I pictured a crowd with raw eggs dripping from their faces. I agreed with his final remark: "I'm celebrating that the Civil Rights Act will let more Negroes vote in the South!"

He agreed when I responded, "It's shameful that Negroes are treated so badly a century after the Civil War ended slavery."

Monday, June 20, 1960: Black and White

Relieved to be done with fair but tough exams, I bought a size 10 black swimsuit, white beach robe, black-and-white boat neck top, and white gloves. Craig and Dominic rewarded me with calls! Forty-five minutes of talk seemed like five!

Thursday, June 23, 1960: Birthday

Did Mom send a card or gift for Sara's forty-third birthday tomorrow? Tempted to make a card, I remembered the rule about no contact until next January and sent nothing.

Saturday, June 25, 1960: Eva

On the phone, Eva said, "Exams were a cinch! The Schuyler intellectual level is so low that harder exams would result in most kids flunking."

I laughed. "If AHS exams get harder, I'll transfer to Schuyler! How's Paul?"

"Irresistibly attractive…Most of us girls have crushes on him. I'm still *persona non grata* to Xavier and Ric."

"They should stop acting nasty! What's their reason?"

"I can only speculate. At Hackett where we were overweight, unathletic outsiders, X called often. We relished books like *The Lonely Crowd*, *The Stranger*, *The Mandarins*, and *No Exit*. Even though we're thinner now, maybe he feels abandoned because I've dated a little and made friends among the dramatics crowd."

"He probably envies your good looks and popularity! At Hackett, you were voted homeroom veep and *most likely to succeed*!"

"Thank you, Angela."

"Slim, cute Ric shouldn't ignore you!"

"Popular Ric is loyal to and influenced by Xavier. X seems to be interested in Paul's girlfriend. I rate his chances at zero unless suave Paul drops her."

We chuckled. "Eva, those four books sound good for summer reading! What did you like about them?"

"They emphasize authenticity, individuality, nonconformity, and freedom."

"Are you dating anyone you like?"

"Although grand passion on either side is missing, I'm grateful to be invited out occasionally by a senior."

"I feel intimidated and get tongue-tied near the only senior I know. Magnetic Parker, the godlike yearbook editor, is in my Latin class. You poised actresses fare better." We giggled.

Sunday, June 26, 1960: Doreen

I was glad to hear from Doreen who asked, "How was the Youth Council picnic at Thacher Park?"

"The tall junior who took me must have left his tongue at home. He played volleyball and softball well, but was silent on our Indian Ladder trail hike. His arm was around me, but he didn't even walk me to the door at the end. Thanks to the nice couple who doubled with us and other kids, I exercised my vocal chords and laughed."

"Angela, I feel sorry for someone shyer than I."

"With shy boys, I can't think of anything to say either. As a listener, I do better with talkers like Yeats. Last night at Bea's Sweet Sixteen party, Yeats and I danced and had fun. Though he briefly kissed my neck and shoulders above my white pique dress, I appreciated that he's a gentleman who didn't go too far in public. He asked me to go steady."

"Wow! What did you say?"

"In shock, I said, 'Thank you for asking me, Yeats. I have a great time on our dates and I like you a lot. I'm too young to settle down with one person. I hope that we can keep going out and having fun.'"

"Did he seem okay?"

"Doreen, I can't tell. I want to avoid hurting his feelings. I tried to say that I'd decline going steady with anyone."

"How're your forbidden boys?"

I giggled. "Recently, Dominic and I had a typical hour phone talk. I've been happy to talk to Craig weekly and spend almost as much time with him as if we were dating."

"Who's your favorite?"

"Your boy-crazy friend adores Yeats, Craig, Dominic, Luke, Hank, Lon, Zeke, and others." We chuckled.

Monday, June 27, 1960: Tennis and Grades

At the Washington Park tennis courts, summery weather in the high eighties felt delightful. I ran into Yeats, who held my hand and walked me home after trouncing me at tennis.

Smiling, Dad looked satisfied with my answer about exams: "My average is 96.67. Geometry was 100, Latin 99, world history 98, English 92, Spanish I 95, and health 96. In Latin, I was surprised to get a *magna cum laude* award for placing seventh at my level in the Eastern Zone Latin Teachers' Association contest!"

Tuesday, June 28, 1960: Paint and Frustration

I like to watch the short, quiet, cute painter, seventeen, as he covers the sandalwood living room walls with off-white paint.

Happy that Yeats called to talk awhile, I wished for a date invitation. Does he feel rejected because I declined going steady? Why don't boys say how they feel?

Wednesday, June 29, 1960: Graduation

As a lowly sophomore, I was excited to be invited to the ninety-second annual commencement at the Palace Theatre. The AHS band played well before and after a Chamber of Commerce leader spoke. I sat with Marcus, winner of the French II prize, and Udeh, who won the German II award. I got the five-dollar Latin II prize for the highest final exam mark, the Latin II civilization prize, and a Latin II reading certificate. When Eva called, I mentioned, "Thirty-six percent of AHS grads got college entrance diplomas."

She quipped, "Schuyler has three-point-six percent." I chuckled before she continued. "Seriously, out of 150 seniors, only twenty or thirteen percent were college-entrance!"

Friday, July 1, 1960: Mrs. E

Tears came as I read Mrs. E's reply to my recent note, thanking her for making history interesting and fun this year.

Dear Angela,

Thank you for your lovely letter. You have been a wonderful student and no teacher could feel more fulfilled than I in watching you grow and reach out for knowledge and information. But more important, you have special gifts of character, for you are a warm, sincere, and honest girl with a rich, unprejudiced mind, at home both in the world of ideas and in the exciting world of people. I know these great gifts will continue to grow and delight all who know you: your parents, your teachers, and your friends. I feel privileged to share with your parents their deep pride and affection for you.

I wish I could have Mrs. E again. Other favorite teachers were Mrs. B for English at Patroon School and Miss K in fourth grade. Following Mrs. E's advice, I'm keeping this tenth-grade activities list for college applications: United Synagogue Youth (USY) at Temple Israel, XEA sorority at the Center, and at AHS: Latin Club, Theta Alpha Literary Society, Forum (current events club), and Junior Red Cross (representative elected by homeroom). This year at AHS has been my best!

Saturday, July 2, 1960: Tennis

Playing tennis Thursday in Washington Park, Doreen and I felt pleased to meet two pleasant boys. Today, Yeats had his parents' car. After our tennis game, during which he helped improve my serve, he treated me to ice cream. What a great time!

I felt happy that Craig and Dominic entertained me for over two hours on the phone. I adore freedom to have summer fun without homework and test fears! With my period here, I must eat lightly and take Midol for the usual cramps.

Sunday, July 3, 1960: In NYC

Our NYC relatives took us out for a lovely lunch at Tavern on the Green in Central Park. Aunt Lila said, "Angela, it's time to think about college only two years away."

Cousin Hal said, "Angela, Columbia has been ideal for me. Though Barnard admission is very competitive, your grades are good enough. I'd like to show you around campus this afternoon."

I smiled. "Thank you!"

Eating pizza after the walking tour, I said to Hal, "I see why this V and T Restaurant is a popular campus hangout. Thank you for treating me and showing me interesting Columbia and Barnard places!"

"You're welcome, Angela! Are you interested in being a Barnard Honeybear?"

I chuckled. "I love bears and want to live in NYC! Thanks to you, Barnard will be my first choice if I get a scholarship. Otherwise, I'll have to attend a state school. I appreciate your help when you're busy studying political science in graduate school." Looking up to sophisticated, intelligent Hal, I felt flattered and grown-up that he made time for me! Sara's only about forty blocks south of Barnard!

Monday, July 4, 1960: Donald

Back in Albany tonight, I was happy to read this from my 1958 Catskill vacation boyfriend: "I will live at home and start Queens College soon. I still plan to major in English and write fiction." I wish Donald's letter had arrived Saturday. I would have called him from Aunt Lila's apartment. I wrote back about my tour of and plan to attend Barnard. I'd love to see Donald again.

Tuesday, July 5, 1960: Dora and Dostoyevsky

I felt lucky to start earning a dollar an hour at the hot, dusty, jam-packed, topsy-turvy Yarn Shop at 26 South Hawk Street! My first paying job is helping Dora Adler pack to move to a big, clean store at 56 Central Avenue.

I cooled off at the Palace Theatre with Eva. The delightful Cole Porter movie musical *Can-Can* starred Shirley MacLaine and Frank Sinatra, whom I enjoyed in *Some Came Running.*

After hearing about my job, Eva shared, "While job-hunting, I'm appreciating English translations of Dostoyevsky's Russian novels. Next, I'll tackle *War and Peace.*"

"The Russian names got too confusing for me to finish the first chapter. But I loved *Anna Karenina* in English class."

Eva replied, "After finding the best translation, I'll make a name chart."

"Why didn't I think of that? Which Dostoyevsky novel is your favorite?"

"I've enjoyed them all in the order they were written: *Notes from the Underground, Crime and Punishment, The Idiot, The Possessed,* and *The Brothers Karamazov.* Surviving years imprisoned at a Siberian work camp, Dostoyevsky was the opposite of an ivory-tower writer!"

"I should be more thankful about how good I have it. Think of brave diarist Anne Frank, who lived in terror hiding from the Nazis before dying in a concentration camp. I'm sad that she missed enjoying her outstanding book's worldwide success."

Wednesday, July 6, 1960: Packing

My doll and I at age four loved the matching aqua wool cardigans with brown leather buttons Mom knit from Dora's yarn and instructions. Older and shorter than Mom, roly-poly Dora has blue eyes and pasty skin without make-up. Grayish brown hair strands straggle from her bun. Dora's wrinkly, faded, cotton-print dresses remind me of Mom's house-cleaning wardrobe. Dora knits so fast that her hands look blurred.

Customers put up with the dirty, crowded, messy store because Dora fixes their worst knitting mistakes and helps them finish the hardest patterns! While a steady stream of customers occupies Dora, I pack, including numbering and labeling cartons and keeping a list. The millions of colors and types of knitting and crochet yarn and embroidery thread, tons of sizes and kinds of needles and hooks, numerous stamped linens, many needlepoint patterns, buttons of all colors and sizes, bolts of trimmings like lace, and illustrated instruction sheets and pamphlets made me ask Dora, "How do you find things?"

She chortled. "Sometimes it takes days and I give up." Having seen her quickly locate merchandise for waiting customers, I enjoyed the sense of humor of the first English person I've met. I tend to listen more to her accent than what she says.

Dora at our 7/4/53, Thacher Park picnic

Thursday, July 7, 1960: Hank and Luke

Last night's temperature of below fifty degrees made this morning's packing cooler. Picturing handsome actor Louis Jordan, I softly sang romantic *Can-Can* songs: *I Love Paris, It's All Right with Me, C'est Magnifique, Let's Do It, Just One of Those Things,* and *You Do Something to Me.*

Yesterday and this afternoon at Washington Park, Doreen and I played tennis with various boys. Smart Hank and Luke were the most fun. Hank, with a NYC accent, is about six feet tall with straight black hair, a hooked nose, acne facial scars, a pear-shaped body, and bowed legs. Good at tennis, he made hilarious comments after our balls went wild or into the net. I laughed until my stomach ached. At Doreen's house, we four kidded and cracked up while playing ping-pong until 11 PM. Elated, I yearned to date these boys. Manly Luke's around five foot ten with an ideal body, dark eyes and hair, and glasses.

Friday, July 8, 1960: Work and Play

Dora said, "During girlhood in London before World War I, I learned to knit and crochet. At your age I got my first job to help support my family." Lack of money kept her from attending nursing school. Mom calls Dora an *old maid*. I'm curious, but afraid to ask whether she was ever slimmer with boyfriends and marriage proposals.

We both sweat, I from packing and she from excess fat. Bothered by her body odor and hoping that my deodorant holds up, I caught myself before rudely blurting, "Do they use deodorant in England?"

Sitting on a stool surrounded by merchandise boxes, Dora ate an apple and read the newspaper. I asked, "How do you feel about urban renewal making you move?"

She chuckled. "I'd rather not budge because moving's hard work, as you know. If I must move, your help before the movers come July 31 makes summer ideal. Customers will prefer a clean, new place." We laughed after she joked, "A miracle might happen. I may keep the new store neater."

Evening tennis with Luke and Hank was exciting! At Doreen's, ping-pong, snacks, and repartee were fun. After the guys left at 1:30 AM, I slept over. Doreen said, "What a great summer!"

"I agree! I'll miss you!"

"I'm usually eager to swim in the lake and meet new people. Not this year..."

"You can stay in our guest room!"

"I'll ask, but my strict father will probably want me in the country with my mother and sister."

Saturday, July 9, 1960: Hank

After hours of tennis, Hank treated me to ice cream at nearby Michael's. I said, "I appreciate your coaching! My tennis has improved."

"You're welcome. You're better coordinated than many girls."

"Thank you. How did you become so good?"

"Though I've practiced since junior high, tennis seems to come easily. Being tall and fairly strong helps. I'd join the AHS team, but only as captain."

I giggled. "Do you like golf?"

"Too boring. Energetic daily tennis lets me read Socrates, Aristotle, Plato, Spinoza, Descartes, Locke, Kant, Hume, Hegel, Kierkegaard, and Nietzsche for hours and eat ice cream without gaining weight," he joked.

"Wow! Aren't those books difficult?"

"Not for anyone intelligent like you."

"Thank you, Hank, but I prefer novels."

"Why do Albany teachers pick the worst novel of each writer for class reading?" Aware of his preference for NYC, I giggled. "Why don't they choose Hardy's *The Return of the Native*, instead of *The Mayor of Casterbridge*, and Wharton's *The House of Mirth* or *The Age of Innocence*, rather than *Ethan Frome*?"

"You're right. Why read Eliot's *Silas Marner*, instead of *Middlemarch*? Eva especially liked Eliot's *Daniel Deronda, The Mill on the Floss,* and *Felix Holt*. Have you read *War and Peace*?"

"After I finish my history and philosophy list..."

Monday, July 11, 1960: Summer Fun

Swimming with my parents yesterday, I enjoyed wearing my first two-piece bathing suit. I'm lucky to have a small waist and stomach which isn't fat.

After work today, tennis with Craig was fun. He let me try riding his boys' bike on the way to Michael's for sodas. We walked to my house and sat on the porch bantering.

At the Center dance, Yeats and three older boys danced with me. Yeats bought me ice cream, took me home, and kissed me goodnight. I enjoyed his company!

Tuesday, July 12, 1960: Note

Nervously gripping the pink vinyl seat of my dining room chair, I bravely said, "I noticed an envelope from Sara in today's mail. What did she write?"

Mom replied, "She thanked me for the birthday card and asked us to avoid contacting her until at least next year."

I asked, "Why?"

"Her therapist advised it. Herm, shall I look for a new suitcase?" I felt too squelched to persist.

Thursday, July 14, 1960: Play

After fun tennis with Luke and Hank, I was thrilled that cool Mike's Log Cabin admitted us three after Hank showed his fake draft card. Hank, who's sixteen, explained, "At eighteen, boys must register for the military draft, so this card I bought proves that I'm old enough to drink this beer." Enjoying the sweet, red Singapore Sling Hank suggested, I felt grown-up but not drunk. Mike's cocktails are weak.

Friday, July 15, 1960: Talk

Dominic called twice for a total of two hours of fun talk!

Saturday, July 16, 1960: Dream

After packing my green suitcase, I went to sleep early. This vivid dream recreated last summer's crisis: Sara rushed into our living room, upset and disheveled after fighting off her attacker and running home from the bus stop. The parents acted skeptical. When Sara turned to me, I did what I should have. After hugging her, I said, "Let's call the police before he escapes. I'm so sorry that you had to go through this, Sara!" Though she looked less upset, she still returned to NYC and stopped communicating with us. Does this dream mean that Sara would have left even if I'd said the right thing?

Sunday, July 17, 1960: Girl Friday

When we passed NYC after speeding south on the NYS Thruway, I wanted to ask Sara's opinion of the emotionally powerful movie I recently saw: *Portrait in Black* with Lana Turner, Anthony Quinn, and Sandra Dee.

Dinner with the Levines at Asbury Park's Metropolitan Hotel included Mom's comments about her NYS Department of Mental Hygiene job: "My job lets me learn about psychology and occupational therapy and work independently in an air-conditioned office at a convenient location." She passed around what Dr. Saper, Director of Psychological Services, wrote:

> One of Mrs. Weiss' exceptional contributions was reorganizing our filing system. While assigned to my office two days a week, she devised a Master Filing Chart called *The Brain*, which won a Merit Award. This saved me valuable time in finding material in files quickly and marking copies for filing. This also greatly helped Dr. Blair when he was first appointed. Mrs. Weiss made a file index booklet to further facilitate locating material. She is a very responsible worker who shows mature, keen judgment. Mrs. Weiss is my idea of a perfect Girl Friday as she is always eager to be of the utmost help and keeps the entire office including bookcases, files, and cabinets in perfect

order. She works at an exceptional level and certainly
deserves the upgrade to Senior Typist.

Dad said, "You deserve more money, Hon!"

Instead of saying that she deserves a downgrade as a
mother for barring her daughter from dating gentiles, I
asked, "How about your skit *The Brain*?"

Mom replied, "New staff find it helpful."

Evelyn said, "Fern, tell us more."

"Only three pages long, it's set in our building at 217
Lark. The characters are my three department heads and
I. Act One shows office chaos prior to *The Brain's* imple-
mentation. In the second and last act, I perform my duties
without continual interruption. With *The Brain*, department
heads easily find their own files."

Karl said, "Pretty creative, Girl Friday!"

Robin, now fourteen, asked, "How long will the
upgrade take?"

Mom replied, "Government wheels turn slowly." Everyone snickered.

Monday, July 18, 1960: Flirting

Last evening after meeting several busboys, I went out with
Jewish Richie, who's eighteen and a senior in Lakewood, NJ.
He kissed my fingertips and my cheek and loaned me his
coat as we walked on the breezy boardwalk until around
11:30. When he tried to make out, I felt annoyed and said
no. What nerve! I just met him.

Today, Richie talked to me at breakfast. Our busboy
Barry chatted while walking me to the beach. Eddie from
our hotel conversed, let me use his sweatshirt, and swam

with me. Back at our hotel, I enjoyed kidding around with Eddie and other bellhops.

Tuesday, July 19, 1960: Playing

Richie chatted, played ping-pong, and swam with me at the pool where the lifeguard and band drummer talked to me. When Richie took me for a walk in the afternoon, I let him hold my hand and put his arm around me. Of course, I refused to make out.

At the pool, I watched boys horse around in the water. Eddie and three boys took Anita, a pleasant teen guest, and me to La Bove for coffee and a long walk. Without showing interest in boys, shy Robin has stayed with our parents.

At the hotel, Richie took me up in the elevator. The pest tried to make out again! Though I accepted a brief good-bye kiss, I kept my mouth closed when he tried to French kiss with *la tongue*. Though he's cute and fun, I hardly know him. Appreciating gentlemen like Yeats, Craig, and Dominic, I wrote them postcards:

> I'm happy that my parents and I are here for a week's vacation! We got our photograph in the Jersey shore magazine *Spotlight*, next to an ad for famous Della Reese, who will soon sing in a local night club! We saw the interesting but scary movie *Psycho* with Janet Leigh and Anthony Perkins. Taking a shower will never be the same!

Left to right: Dad, Mom, me, Robin, Evelyn, & Karl, courtesy of Spotlight Magazine

Wednesday, July 20, 1960: Harvey

I declined an invite to Belmar beach from the drummer because Aunt Lila and Cousin Ron visited from NYC. We're worried about Uncle Harvey, hospitalized with cancer.

After our relatives left, Rafi from Israel chatted at the pool, took me for a walk, and treated me at a café with Irish singing. I listened to Rafi, a pretty interesting talker, on the walk back and by the pool.

Every night before I fall asleep, I say the *Shema Yisrael* prayer, which means, "Hear, oh Israel: the Lord our God, the Lord is one." Tonight, I prayed for poor Uncle Harvey.

Thursday, July 21, 1960: Rafi and Pete

After swimming and talking to Rafi and the lifeguards all morning at the pool, I went to the beach with Rafi. We swam and took a long beach walk with his arm around me.

At the hotel, I enjoyed a long talk in simple, slow Spanish with a South American: Jewish Pete, twenty-one and entering City College in NYC.

Though Rafi invited me to play miniature golf, I was having too much fun talking and playing ping-pong with two NYC boys. One recently graduated from Cousin Ron's Bronx High School of Science, which has only super-smart kids.

I prayed for God to save Uncle Harvey.

Friday, July 22, 1960: Gantry

After I swam with four boys, Rafi treated me to miniature golf and an absorbing, dramatic movie, *Elmer Gantry*, which we discussed with Pete at the hotel. I said, "Burt Lancaster and Shirley Jones acted so well that I cried at the end."

"Religion should be ethical," said Rafi. "I'm glad Jews don't try to convert people, like the evangelists in the movie."

Startled, I asked, "Don't synagogue leaders charging members high dues act greedy like those evangelists?"

"I must see the movie," said Pete. These gentlemen discussing interesting subjects attract me more than Richie pressuring me to make out.

Yeats' friendly letter signed *Love* pleasantly surprised me. I hope he asks me out!

Saturday, July 23, 1960: Mambo, Merengue

My last full day here was a blast, including repartee at the pool with a dozen boys. They showed off by stealing trousers and trying to push a guy in the pool. These NYC boys make me laugh more than most Albany boys.

After dinner, Anita and I learned chess from and bantered with nine boys, including Pete, Barry, Rafi, and Richie. Eddie said, "You look smooth with your tan in that white dress, even better than your photo in *Spotlight*." I felt myself blush as I thanked him. At 2 AM, too excited to sleep after a fabulous evening, I wrote Doreen and Eva postcards:

> I'm having the greatest time here flirting with loads of fun boys working at our hotel. Tonight, I watched the hotel entertainment and danced the mambo, tango, merengue, cha cha, bolero, foxtrot, and jitterbug with terrific dancers Pete from Colombia and Eddie! See you later, alligator!
>
> Love, Angela

I prayed for Uncle Harvey.

Sunday, July 24, 1960: Goodbyes

After a fun morning with several guys at the pool, I went around saying goodbye to Anita and the others. After a bell-hop removed the splinter in my finger, he said, "I wanted to take you out but you were always accounted for. Can you return for a weekend? We could have a great time in NYC at the Rainbow Room!"

"Thank you. It sounds like fun, but I have to stay home and work the rest of the summer." He kissed me goodbye. After Richie, Eddie, and Pete took my address and said goodbye, Barry and two bellboys kissed me goodbye.

I came down from cloud nine at the NYC hospital. It doesn't look good for nice Uncle Harvey. Poor Aunt Rhoda has no kids to comfort her!

1958: Aunt Rhoda, Cousin Ron, & Uncle Harvey

Monday, July 25, 1960: Kirk

Mail from the rabbi's son Frankie and Cousin Ron's friend perked me up.

On the bus, I said to Rex, "I'm going to the movie *Strangers When We Meet*."

"It stars my uncle Kirk Douglas."

"Have you seen it?"

"Our family sees all his movies and will see it soon, though it's not Kirk's favorite. How's your aunt whom I met, the one who dated Kirk in Amsterdam?"

"What a good memory! I miss Sara, back in NYC for the last year." I changed the subject to his summer activities.

Kirk's romantic movie, which also starred Kim Novak, was good. On the bus home, cute Lon kept me company.

At the Center, I enjoyed dancing with Luke, Yeats, and others. Yeats accompanied me to Doreen's, where ping-pong with her and JP was fun. After Yeats' goodnight kiss, I felt less let down after my glorious vacation and sad visit to Uncle Harvey.

Tuesday, July 26, 1960: Doubles

After work, Luke and I played doubles tennis with Doreen and JP, who drove us in his snazzy red convertible to Joe's for snacks! At Doreen's, we four had many ping-pong laughs with the ball going wild before JP took us home.

Sunday, July 30, 1960: Letter

I sent this today:

Dear Ron,

How's Uncle Harvey? Please give him my hug. I pray that he'll get better. You must be spending every day at the hospital, helping Aunt Rhoda.

My enjoyable week included two movies: *The Apartment* with Jack Lemmon and Shirley MacLaine, very sweet, and the hilarious British comedy *Carry on Nurse*.

With friends still looking for summer jobs, I'm thankful to earn money for college. Friday, the moving company picked up the store counters and fixtures plus zillions of cartons of merchandise I packed. Even though the new store isn't air conditioned, unpacking every morning for the next three weeks should be easier.

Love, Angela

Monday, August 1, 1960: Paul

Doreen and JP kindly drove me to the Center in his fun car with the top down. I was thrilled to talk to Paul, as entrancing as ever. When he slow danced with me about four times, I closed my eyes to savor every electrifying second. Strong leader (which I like) Hank and I danced about five times. Herb, a tall, amusing AHS senior, danced with me and said, "I'll call you."

Friday, August 5, 1960: Ina

Craig called! Learning that I too had seen *From the Terrace*, he asked, "What did you think of Ina Balin?"

"I liked her, Paul Newman, and Joanne Woodward."

"Ina is more beautiful than Joanne. She looks like you."

"Thank you! What a great compliment! Ina's part seemed more sympathetic. Paul Newman must prefer Joanne, his real-life wife." I tactfully avoided gushing about the actor's dreamy blue eyes.

Saturday, August 6, 1960: Cool

Tonight, Yeats escorted me to a fun beatnik house party. Dressed in black turtlenecks and black jeans, we smiled at the sign on the door: *Greenwich Village*. Someone read out loud poems from Lawrence Ferlinghetti's book *A Coney Island of the Mind*.

Afterwards, a kid said, "Don't you *dig* old Lawrence?"

Classmate Marcus replied, "Ferlinghetti isn't strictly a beat poet," and read Allen Ginsberg's poem, *A Supermarket in California.*

"Cool, man!" exclaimed some of the kids. Yeats and I chuckled before I said, "These poems are good!"

Looking at my eyes encircled with heavy black liner, Yeats flirted. "I'm under the spell of your big brown eyes!"

I smiled. "It's cool to be with a cool beatnik with a cool black beret!"

He chuckled. "Would you like to go out Thursday evening?"

"I'd love to, but I'll be at Tanglewood with my parents."

Pleased that Yeats finally asked me out, I wish he'd chosen another day. I felt sad about this anniversary of the Sara crisis.

Monday, August 8, 1960: Harvey

At the Center, I was elated to talk to Paul for a while before being invited to play ping-pong with three other boys. One said, "You look eighteen," which made me happy! Two of them drove me to the house of Zeke (Casanova!). Trying to learn chess from Zeke and the others was fun.

Hearing that my uncle died, I felt disappointed that God didn't save such a good person. In 1956, Aunt Rhoda and Uncle Harvey sent my first real diary with a lock and key.

Sunday, August 14, 1960: Mourning

Today, sitting *shiva* in Aunt Rhoda's NYC living room with Ron, Hal, and our parents was very sad. Synagogue friends brought home-cooked food and expressed sympathy. Poor Aunt Rhoda broke down several times. Fortunately, her closest friend Aunt Lila lives nearby.

In NYC, Sara was on my mind. Doesn't Mom miss her only sister? She and Dad were quiet on the return train. While reading *The Leopard*, a historical novel about Sicily, I daydreamed about kissing Paul, who was born there.

1931: Mom's Essex car behind Mom, 19, & Sara, 14

Tuesday, August 16, 1960: End in Sight

During the dinner I made of frozen fish sticks and salad, Mom said, "Angela, Dora said that your hard work has been a big help. Will everything be arranged in the new store by Friday?"

"I hope so." I chuckled. "You'd think I'd be a better knitter after 120 hours with Dora, but packing and unpacking took all my time. Dora's talk to customers and me was never boring. Unlike most women, she tells her age: fifty-five. Arriving in NYC before World War II, she lived in the Bronx on 176th Street in a rooming house for unmarried women. Dad, weren't you born in the Bronx?"

"Yes. Dolly, do you remember the Bronx Zoo when you were four?"

"Sort of. Dora's glad to have her own Albany apartment and store. She enjoys doing and teaching needlework."

"Did she mention her Ohio rabbi brother?" Mom inquired.

"Vaguely."

Dad said, "We appreciate your saving everything you earned. Is your one-dollar weekly allowance enough?" I nodded yes and smiled after Dad commented, "Boys treating you on dates lets us manage on less."

Wednesday, August 17, 1960: Calls

This week, Craig has been calling. Tonight, two hours on the phone with Dominic whizzed by. I'm happy that this summer has been perfect, except for Harvey.

Thursday, August 18, 1960: Famous

While we ate sandwiches on the Tanglewood lawn before a great Gershwin concert, Mom said, "The steno pool made a big fuss about my picture in the *Civil Service Leader* newspaper." Dad read the clipping out loud:

> Suggestion Pays Off. Mrs. Fern Weiss, a typist in the NYS Department of Mental Hygiene, is being congratulated by Dr. Paul Hoch, left, commissioner, after receiving a merit award for a suggestion to revise an annual report form. The suggestion, which simplified tabulation, resulted in man-hour savings both in the central office and throughout the department's twenty-seven institutions. Looking on are Daniel Shea, secretary to the department, second from right, and Dr. Charles Niles, assistant commissioner.

We laughed when Dad said, "We're lucky to live with a celebrity who hobnobs with top dogs and gets free Tanglewood tickets!"

Mom said, "Pauline kindly said, 'Thanks to you, all those highly paid people can skip wrangling over the Occupational Therapy Services' annual report for days.'"

I said, "Congratulations on saving the state time and tax money!"

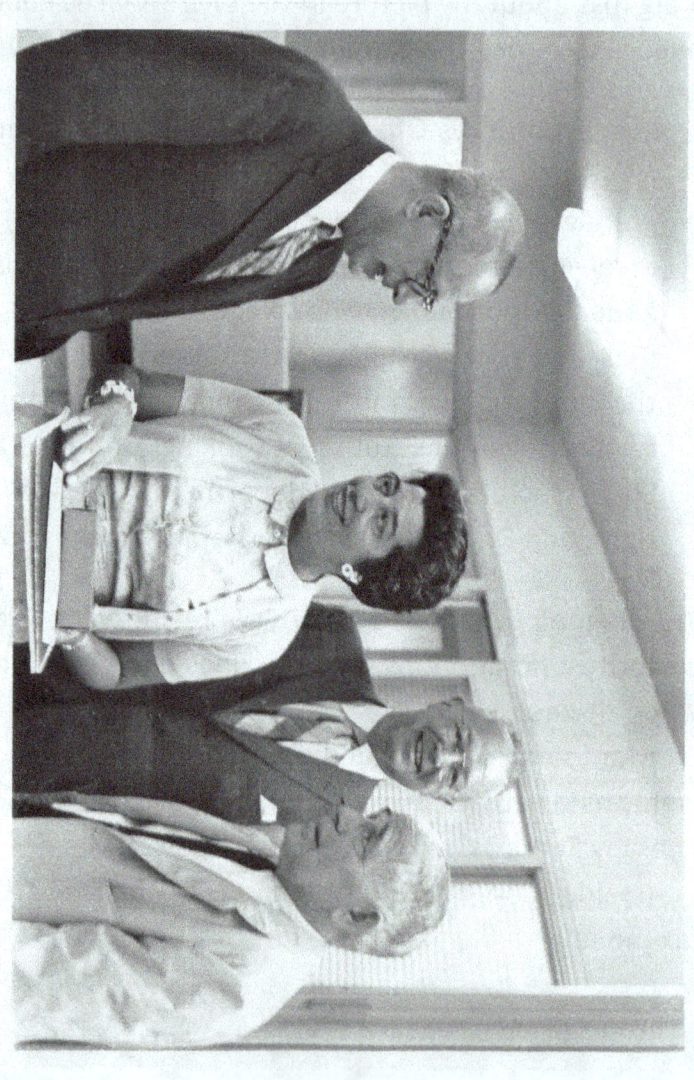

Mom

Friday, August 19, 1960: Absolute Blast

Craig took me to Dominic's fabulous house party! Joking around and dancing every song with Craig, Dominic, and charming Paul were the most! On the way home, Craig agreed when I said, "That party was terrific, especially the twist, stroll, lindy, and slow dances!"

"Can you come with our group to the three-county fair?" Craig asked.

"I'd love to! I'll ask my parents!"

Saturday, August 20, 1960: County Fair

At the fair in Altamont ten miles west of Albany, Dominic, Craig, intriguing Zeke, Eva, and I saw prize-winning farm animals. I laughed at my friends' banter:

Dominic: "This hog forgot her bath."

Craig: "And her deodorant has worn off."

Eva: "I wish I'd brought cologne to lend her."

After riding the carousel, we strolled past midway booths where the boys tried to win stuffed animals. Craig took me on the huge Ferris wheel at sunset. Gazing at the beautiful green country view for miles around, I said, "I wonder how far we can see."

The record hop where I danced with Craig and Dominic was the most fun. At my house, we five danced to records and wisecracked on the porch. Jewish Zeke's presence kept my parents from objecting. The last two evenings have been perfect!

Wednesday, August 24, 1960: Hudson

Craig's handsome dad took him, Dominic, Eva, and me for terrific boating on the wide, calm Hudson River near Albany! Craig had his arm around me and we held hands before he took me for an exhilarating boat ride alone. At his house, the four of us talked, snacked, and listened to records. I loved dancing with AHS's Fred Astaire, Craig. His father drove us home after a fab time!

Friday, August 26, 1960: Boys

Donald's delightful letter from Queens arrived before I talked to Dominic for a half hour. Jewish Jed from Dominic's party asked me out. With brown hair and eyes and glasses, he's my age and slightly taller than I.

Saturday, August 27, 1960: Jed

Jed took me to *Ocean's 11*, an okay movie, at the Strand Theatre. I liked talented singer Frank Sinatra and excellent dancer Sammy Davis Jr. We had spumoni ice cream and pizza at the Moon. Though I had a nice time and Jed's a good egg, I said no when he tried to kiss me goodnight. He's like a pal.

Monday, August 29, 1960: Center

On a sunny day with a ninety-two-degree high, Jed took me to the Center. After ping-pong, I had fun because Jed's a good dancer. His older brother drove us for ice cream on Western Avenue. Jed's goodnight kiss was surprisingly good. At the Center, I enthusiastically accepted Herb's invite, while we danced, to the upcoming ABG Jewish fraternity weekend! I wish that this ideal summer could last forever.

Wednesday, August 31, 1960: Kisser

After a half-hour phone talk with Dominic, Jed escorted me to a party where we danced a lot and I conversed with the host about music. During boring TV at Jed's house, I avoided his ungentlemanly attempts to kiss me in front of his friend! After Jed's brother drove us to my house, Jed kissed me goodnight several times, long and good. I have to admit that he can kiss, but I prefer Craig's and Dominic's personalities and manners.

Thursday, September 1, 1960: Party

At a party, I talked and danced a lot with an overweight boy, who took another couple and me to the Boulevard in a cute, turquoise Nash convertible. Though our group had fun, I declined a movie invite because I'm attracted only to boys with the self-control to avoid being fat. I declined Jed's invite to his house to avoid boring TV and necking attempts.

Saturday, September 3, 1960: Frat Party

Last night felt like fall (ugh!) with a low of forty-three. I was glad that the day warmed up to over seventy. To kick off the ABG fraternity weekend, Herb took me to JP's house party where I enjoyed hearing about Doreen's country fun. When Herb tried to put his head in my lap as we sat on a couch talking, I pulled away. My annoyed look said, "You're weird!"

Sunday, September 4, 1960: Good Sport

I love the gorgeous dozen white rosebuds the florist delivered! After I thanked Herb, he took me by cab to the Ten Eyck Hotel for dancing. Dancing with Luke was like frosting on the cake! We sat with Herb's friends. Herb had his arm around me and kissed me on the cheek in the cab to Joe's. At JP's house party, everyone was making out. Feeling uncomfortable, I wanted to leave but tried to be a good sport. Moving away when Herb again put his head in my lap, I let him kiss my face and lips once with my mouth open. He returned me home in a taxi and kissed me goodnight. I appreciated being taken to the dance. As a good date, I tried to make the best of the evening, despite exasperation about being stuck with fast Jews rather than smarter, gentlemanly gentiles.

1960 AHS Junior

The three great essentials to achieve anything worthwhile are…hard work, stick-to-itiveness, (and) common sense.

Thomas A. Edison

Wednesday, September 7, 1960: Subjects and Bragging

Unsure about my common sense, I'll need persevering diligence in Latin III, intermediate algebra, advanced American history, advanced English, and Spanish II.

Dominic's call cheered me up. After I talked to Jed, Mom answered the next call. "Angela, it's Udeh." Though unathletic and shorter than I with prominent ears, popular Udeh's warm positive personality, top grades, and extracurricular activities made him our class president. After I answered his homework question, we said goodbye.

Dad's falsetto mimicked Udeh's mom's pompous bragging at our synagogue. "My Udeh got a hundred *As*! My Udeh won every prize! My Udeh will soon be President of our country." Although laughs escaped me, I wished Dad were more tolerant. I felt sorry for a widow working full-time, paying for everything on her NYS clerical salary, and saving for college for Udeh, who's probably her only joy.

The advantage of parents who always criticize me is avoiding embarrassment: they never boast.

Saturday, September 10, 1960: Two Dates

Yesterday, Jed drove me to his house for TV and Scrabble, a game I enjoy. When his brother drove us for ice cream, I staved off Jed's make-out attempts.

Today, after my phone chat with Dominic, Jed took me to the elegant Hellman Theatre for an interesting movie, *Sons and Lovers*, based on a novel by famous D. H. Lawrence. Saying, "I plan to read the book," I wanted Jed to intelligently discuss the movie, instead of boring me with TV. After kissing me in the car while his brother drove us to my house, Jed said, "I like you a lot!" Always honest, I stayed silent.

Sunday, September 11, 1960: Olympics

Reading the paper, Dad commented, "Americans won the most Olympic medals! Negro Wilma Rudolf is the fastest female on earth with three gold medals, including the 100-meter race. Negro decathlete Rafer Johnson won the gold!"

As a sports and Olympics fan, I asked, "Why are Negroes better?"

Dad answered, "Not all Negroes are outstanding competitors. Most groups, including Jews, have talented athletes. Most American Negroes are descended from slaves. Though slave traders chose the fittest African tribal people to work long hours on hot plantations, many died young. Those who survived and had kids were a physically elite group."

"That makes sense. Dad, which athletes are Jewish?"

"Dolph Schayes is a top basketball player. In football, Benny Friedman, Sid Luckman, and Marshall Goldberg starred as quarterbacks. Al Rosen and Hank Greenberg excelled in baseball. Max Baer, Barney Ross, and Benny Leonard were standout boxers. Dick Savitt made his mark in tennis."

"Wow! Dad, how about women?"

"Lillian Copeland and Bobbie Rosenfeld were Olympic track and field stars. Agnes Keleti won a slew of gymnastics medals at the last two Olympics. I heard that Olympic gymnastics star Mariya Goro-something (a long Russian name I can't remember) may be Jewish. Angela, you can be proud of your Jewish heritage."

Pleased to hear about Jewish athletes, I wanted to ask whether these stars, as teens, were free to date non-Jews.

Saturday, September 17, 1960: Happy

After a week of phone conversations with Luke (one hour), Craig (ninety minutes), and Dominic (two hours), Julia's party at her house near Whitehall Road was wonderful! Though I missed Eva (busy with her family), I chatted with her Schuyler classmates Ric and Alice.

Julia was sweet to have birthday cupcakes for Tara, who turns sweet sixteen tomorrow! Tara, Julia, Doreen, Marsha, and I reminisced about the good old days in Girl Scouts and at Patroon School. I hugged Tara and gave her a birthday card I made.

Dancing with masculine Dominic and smooth Craig was exciting! When I congratulated Craig on being elected treasurer of the AHS Forum, he chortled. "Managing ten total dollars of dues should be a cinch. Congratulations on winning secretary, Angela!"

"Thank you. Writing meeting minutes is easier than coming up with current events topics, like program chairman Marcus."

"Though he'll have more work than president Yeats, Marcus knows everything from reading the NY Times daily."

I laughed. "Craig, how does he have time for school or anything else? NY Times current events for history class and fun parts like the magazine, book reviews, and crossword puzzle take me all day Sunday!"

"Marcus probably reads fast...I'd rather dance!" He spun and dipped me for the rest of the evening, as kids yelled, "Go Fred and Ginger!" Euphoric, I kept beaming while he took me home and kissed me goodnight!

Julia

Saturday, September 24, 1960: Kissing

Dominic made my week fun by calling almost daily and sitting with me at an evening school meeting! Why did two boys as smart as I, Luke and Udeh, call yesterday about homework? I wish that Luke liked me romantically.

Expecting dancing, I regretted attending tonight's tacky public necking party with Jed. Feeling uncomfortable, good sport Angela allowed a few smooches. I want to kiss only a regular boyfriend I like in private!

Sunday, September 25, 1960: Schuyler

On the phone, Eva said, "Guess who won Schuyler veep. Paul and Ric ran."

I laughed. "If Ric still ignores you, I'll say charismatic Paul."

"Right! Paul seems to prefer Cardinal McCloskey Memorial High School girls to his long-term Schuyler sweetheart."

"Eva, I wish Paul had the good taste to date you! Does Xavier still ignore you?"

"Yes."

"That's disappointing. How're you feeling about it?"

"Angela, it's lasted so long that I mind less. Fortunately, I've made other friends."

"Eva, it's his loss!

Tuesday, September 27, 1960: Miss M

When Eva called, I asked, "Who's your favorite teacher?"

"Our dramatics teacher from NYC! With a hardy laugh and expressive loud voice, Miss M's livelier than other female faculty. Picture Rosalind Russell in *Auntie Mame*."

"She sounds like fun!"

Friday, September 30, 1960: Dominic and John Fitzgerald K

This week, Frankie walked me home once and Luke, Craig, Jed, and Dominic phoned.

Tonight, dinner guest Dominic impressed my parents by drying dishes I washed, playing classical music on our piano, and praising Senator Kennedy's Schenectady speech! When Dad asked what Dom liked about yesterday's speech, he answered, "I agree with Kennedy's remarks about the economy." Dad's thick eyebrows went up when Dom pulled out a newspaper copy and read:

> We have this tremendous industrial capacity in the United States which has been stimulated by automation, which has been stimulated by great capital investments in the last 10 years, and the question is, can we consume in this country and around the world all that we can produce. If we can, we can maintain full employment. If we cannot, we will have layoffs, and it is a somber economic fact that in the United States in 1960, only 2 years after the recession of 1958, we are using only 50 percent of the capacity of our steel mills. Steel is basic to the economy of the United States. If steel is down, then the economy of the United States is on a plateau. Therefore, I consider the most serious domestic problem facing the next administration...the maintenance of full employment.
>
> The high interest rate policy followed by this administration intensified the recession of 1958.
>
> The failure of the Congress and the administration to agree on an area redevelopment bill, which would be of particular benefit in attracting new industry

into communities like Schenectady...is most unfortu-
nate...even if you build the economy of the country
as a unit, you are going to find areas which, because
of technological changes, because of changes in the
use of raw materials...will be left aside...You know all
about that in this section of New York.

When you buy a house, the interest rates you pay
on that house are affected by national policy. I want
to make that national policy more effective.

Seeing my parents smile and nod, Dom continued in his
strong voice, "I admire that Kennedy's a student of history
who applies its lessons to the present."

Dad said, "Impressive!" I hope Dad meant Dom as well
as Kennedy's speech. After thanking Dom for the clipping, I
enjoyed his company at synagogue services.

Dom smiled. "Am I the first Greek Orthodox in these hal-
lowed halls?"

Entranced by his cute dimples, I giggled. "Probably."

Saturday, October 1, 1960: Jake

Today's highlight was a call from smart, amusing Jake, who's
taller than I and cute with a dark blond crew cut. "Angela,
I must be the only AHS Catholic. The rest are in parochial schools."

"Was AHS your preference?"

"Mine and my parents. My intelligent Polish mom wants
my younger brother and me to think for ourselves. My Irish
dad is flexible and more liberal than most Catholics. We go
to church and believe in God, but enjoy getting to know
people of all backgrounds."

"I am impressed and feel the same way. Though my parents' friends are Jewish, I wish I could date gentiles. Intelligence and interesting, fun personalities are more important to me than the same religion."

"I can date non-Catholics...if I ever get up the nerve to ask out a girl."

I giggled. "Jake, you're funny! Parties, school events, and group outings let me be with boys I can't formally date." I can't help but enjoy Jake and feel thankful for good times with Craig and Dominic, despite my family's intolerance.

Tonight, a fun Temple Israel dance with Jed preceded dull TV at his house.

Jake

Sunday, October 2, 1960: Schenectady

After reading the NY Times, I learned this new history from Dominic's clipping about Kennedy's excellent speech!

> The old city of Schenectady was wiped out by an Indian massacre early in its history...the settlers in Schenectady knew about the coming Indian attack over two years in advance...the summer before, they made preparations for resisting it, but they did not believe it would come in the winter. Therefore, they lay down in the winter and the attack came and they were wiped out...there is a somber lesson... those who feel that they are secure, those who are not willing to work in the summer and in the winter, those who are not willing to prepare themselves for hard days ahead, have suffered in history the inevitable result.
>
> I think the United States is going to pass more difficult times in 1961, 1962, 1963, and 1964. The next President of the United States is going to have to meet a crisis in Berlin...He is going to have to meet a position in the Formosa Straits with an increasingly dangerous and belligerent Chinese communist government...The job of the next President will be more difficult...than it has been in any administration since the time of Lincoln.
>
> But in the last four years I have traveled to every State in the Union...and I have the greatest possible confidence in it. We have a productive strength which is unequaled. We have a form of government which every person in the world...would most like to

live under, given their free choice. We represent, in my judgment, the way of the future...if there is any lesson of the last ten years in history...what is it? The desire to be free and independent...ultimately the communist experiment is bound to fail...the United States has lost its image around the world as a friend of freedom. We have often allied ourselves with dictatorships which are on the way out...Thomas Jefferson said the disease of liberty is catching...I want it to spread the world over.

Friday, October 7, 1960: Yeats

Downtown, I smiled after running into Yeats, who walked me up the street. When I asked, "How do you like being a senior?" he kind of shrugged. Wanting to be respected as a lady, I've waited patiently to be asked out without acting forward and saying anything. I sighed at the thought that he probably has a new girlfriend.

Happy that Luke and Dominic have phoned often, I rush to finish homework and chores so I can talk at length. Laughing with entertaining friends rewards me for working hard the rest of the time, especially on intermediate algebra, which I like less than geometry.

Friday, October 14, 1960: Surprise

Dominic's sixteenth birthday party was fabulous! When he walked in the door and twenty friends yelled, "Surprise," he turned beet red and held back tears. I like that he's emotional. His passion comes through when he plays the piano and talks. He and I danced a lot, sat and talked, and held hands. Wiggling around, he said, "My back itches where I can't reach."

I giggled. "Shall I scratch it as a birthday present?"

He turned crimson. "That would be heavenly!" While I scratched, his exaggerated moans and groans cracked me up. The whole evening was the most with his arm often around me! Dancing with Craig and others was a special bonus!

Saturday, October 15, 1960: Indian Summer

Temperatures in the mid-seventies the last two days kept me grinning! After fast housecleaning, I eagerly read *To Kill a Mockingbird*, a woman writer's moving novel about a young girl growing up in the bigoted South.

Friday, October 21, 1960: Walked Home

After a delightful week of almost daily calls from Dominic and occasional calls from Luke and Udeh, I enjoyed being escorted home by Jake, who kept me laughing.

Saturday, October 22, 1960: Birthday

I delivered my sweet sixteen card and gift of a scarf to Doreen. I'm glad that JP will take her dancing tonight!

Tuesday, October 25, 1960: Upgrade

Mom said, "Mr. McAllister, Director of Mental Hygiene Education Services, smiled and said, 'I typed this myself to surprise you.'"

Dad read it out loud:

Special commendation goes to Mrs. Fern Weiss, Typist, Grade 3, who has shown devotion and interest in her work far beyond the demands of the job. Having developed an interest in the educational aspects of the department's program, Mrs. Weiss asked to visit a state school. Unfortunately, department policy did not permit allowing time for this purpose, although permission was requested. On May 6, 1960, Mrs. Weiss used a vacation day and on October 12, 1960, she used her holiday to travel to Rome State School. Her genuine interest in her work exceeds that ordinarily expected; this attitude should be commended.

Mom said, "He forwarded the Grade 7 Senior Typist promotion package with his, Dr. Saper's, and Mrs. McGrath's write-ups; my three-page description of my occupational therapy (OT) duties; and copies of the OT newsletters I wrote, designed, and illustrated in color for statewide distribution. After thanking him, I said, 'Mr. McAllister, I'll be back with your afternoon milk shake in a jiffy.'"

Monday, October 31, 1960: 1956 Girl

For Halloween, I squeezed into the elastic waistband of my old turquoise felt poodle skirt, which I topped with a cardigan over a white blouse. Doreen said, "Your pop-it-bead bracelet and rosebud headband are perfect for 1956." Appreciating other classmates' compliments, I enjoyed touching the curly fur of the black poodle on a rhine-stone leash.

Thursday, November 3, 1960: Lincoln

On the phone, Eva said, "I fervently hope that Kennedy wins. The voting age should be fifteen."

Giggling, I agreed. "Eva, you would have liked Marcus's AHS Forum Lincoln election program."

"In 1860 without radio and TV, Honest Abe must have waited days for results."

"I was surprised to hear, 'Lincoln got a victory telegram at midnight.'"

Eva remarked, "Our best president, Republican Lincoln, won only because slavery issues split the more power-ful Democrats."

"Marcus ran a contest to guess the percentage results of Lincoln and opponents. Great reader Hank came clos-est and was pleased to win Bruce Catton's book, *A Stillness at Appomattox*."

"What were the answers?"

"I'm picturing the blackboard...Lincoln won seventeen states, Breckinridge eleven southern states, and Douglas and Bell five. The popular vote was about forty percent for Lincoln, thirty for Douglas, twenty for Breckinridge, and Bell the rest. Almost sixty percent of electoral votes were for Lincoln. Breckinridge had twenty-four percent, Douglas four, and Bell thirteen."

"Angela, does your photographic memory help on exams?"

"Only for a day or so before it fades...I hope that Kennedy follows in Lincoln's footsteps."

In the famous quotation book Sara left here, Lincoln's "I'm a success today because I had a friend who believed in me and I didn't have the heart to let him down," reminded me of Sara's belief in me.

Sunday, November 6, 1960: Fears

I was surprised and pleased to be one of seven *Knickerbocker News* guest editorial contest winners for the second year! My annoyance about the public's ignorant fears of an intelligent, Harvard-educated Catholic like Kennedy taking orders from the Pope inspired me to write this:

Faiths Will Make the US Strong

Religious prejudice is a horrible thing. Webster's dictionary defines prejudice as an opinion adverse to anything without just grounds or before sufficient knowledge. This definition is precise in that no grounds exist for religious prejudice, which is seldom found in those with sufficient knowledge of other religions. Prejudice is an outgrowth of ignorance. Only education can wipe out ignorance. Hence, we must educate to destroy religious bias.

Why must we even concern ourselves with ways to fight religious bigotry when we live in a country which guarantees religious freedom in its Bill of Rights? Not only is religious prejudice morally wrong, but we appear hypercritical to the rest of the world when we champions of freedom and justice permit religion to be a presidential election issue. We might as well say to countries looking to us for leadership, "Do as we say, not as we do."

Through education and understanding, we can eradicate the evil of religious prejudice from our American way of life. Children must be taught respect and tolerance for other religions, first at home by parents and then in school by teachers.

All of us should try to learn about other religions. We can read books about other faiths. We can discuss religion with friends of different faiths. We can visit places of worship of various religions. Ways can be found if we sincerely want to rid our minds of the scourge of religious bigotry.

This is not a problem that just a few must fight; we must all work against it, for it spreads like a contagious disease. Parents give the disease to children. Children carry it to friends. Friends pass it on and intolerance grows.

We must be thankful that most of us have a religion. We must be grateful that each presidential candidate has a religion to give him the strength and courage in guiding our country that is necessary in such trying and troubled times. For faith, or rather faiths, will make the United States triumphant in our struggle against the godless communist world.

Monday, November 7, 1960: Jackie

Not only do I adore Kennedy, but his wife Jackie is a role model. Dressed in tasteful, simple clothing, she's an intelligent French major who has worked as a writer and excels at riding horses. Jackie and I have the same role model: wonderful actress Audrey Hepburn, a former ballet dancer! Though Jackie's now pregnant, she and Audrey have slim figures which I admire. Both prove that brunettes can be as beautiful as blondes like Marilyn Monroe.

Tuesday, November 8, 1960: Loss

AHS's football team had five victories with four shut-outs until today's 7-18 upset by CBA (Christian Brothers Academy). Sitting between Dominic and Jake in the bleachers, I tried to stop shivering. Today's high was only forty-three degrees with a low of twenty. I laughed at Jake's comment, "Maybe God will right everything with a Kennedy presidential win."

I asked, "How can voters want a sleazy politician like Nixon as president?"

Jake remarked, "Angela, your winning editorial is good enough to tip the scales for Kennedy."

"Thank you, Jake. I'm moving in with Montreal relatives if Nixon wins."

Dominic added, "After Adlai Stevenson lost, I was tempted to live with relatives in Greece during the reactionary Eisenhower years."

"I'm glad you stayed!" I said playfully. He blushed.

At the bowling alley, my lifetime high of 122 left me elated! Dominic, Marie, and I laughed when Jake said: "I love the new use for TV from *The Viewer* newspaper column: forcing traffic law violators to watch bad TV videotapes in a sound-proof glass booth at City Hall. Here's a sample punishment: twenty-four hours with tapes of three-year-old Democratic and Republican paid political messages."

Wednesday, November 9, 1960: Relief

Last night after midnight, I was wide awake in bed listening to radio election coverage in the dark. In the wee hours, I was overjoyed hearing that my hero won! Relieved to avoid living in colder Canada, I finally fell asleep. After school when Craig called, we agreed that Kennedy will be perfect!

Thursday, November 10, 1960: Corning

My parents are down on the crooked O'Connell Democratic machine which has kept Corning mayor since before I was born. After finishing the delicious lamb chop I broiled, I pointed to the Albany newspaper excerpts from his speeches. "I love Corning's remarks about Kennedy's intelligence, courage, knowledge, and vision. Corning seems smart and concerned about urban problems."

Dad replied, "As a Yale Phi Beta Kappa graduate with history and English majors, he has brains. Speechwriters can make politicians sound like saints."

"Dad, Corning mentioned a recent *Sales Management Magazine* business activity forecast. A survey of 308 American cities ranked Albany third of US cities its size and thirteenth overall."

"Angela, statistics may be misleading. If O'Connell doesn't own that magazine, he may have paid a bribe or bought ads in it."

"Dad, Corning said that Albany's business growth is higher than Schenectady's and Troy's combined, even though Albany's population is 20,000 lower."

Mom commented, "That's not saying much. Troy has been going downhill for years. With railroads and ALCO (American Locomotive Company) declining, Schenectady has only GE (General Electric) jobs."

When Luke called, he voiced similar doubts about the survey and Corning's character. Unsure what to think, I'd value Sara's opinion.

Wednesday, November 16, 1960: PSAT

I'm happy about scoring in the ninety-ninth percentile on the PSAT (preliminary scholastic aptitude test)! My scores, 72(0) verbal and 70(0) math, make me less worried about scholarships. I must keep working hard and learning vocabulary.

Friday, November 18, 1960: Rand

Seeing *The Night of January 16th* at AHS with Craig, Jake, and two classmates was a blast. Ayn Rand's play was fun because jurors for the murder trial came from our audience. Whether they voted guilty or not changed the trial outcome and play ending. After a snack at the Boulevard, we five enjoyed many laughs on a Central Avenue walk!

In Sara's quotation book, I liked this: "The hardest thing to explain is the glaringly evident which everybody has decided not to see," from Rand's novel *The Fountainhead*. She came to the US from Russia in 1926.

Wednesday, November 23, 1960: Holiday Week

Calls from Craig, Dominic, and Jake and two days off school kept me beaming all week. I told Jake, "You'd make a great comedian, but someone as brainy as you, especially in math, might prefer something intellectual."

"Angela, thanks for the compliments! I'm thinking of RPI (Rensselaer Polytechnic Institute) for engineering. Do you and your family like hockey?"

"The Olympics hockey gold medal was exciting!"

"My family landed tickets to the RPI hockey tournament in Troy after Christmas! Coach Harkness has produced winning teams almost every year. In 1954, RPI was the division one national champion. In 1958, the team was second in the Tri-State League and hosted the NCAA Frozen Four championship tournament. Last year, they were second in their league with fifteen wins in twenty-one games. This year's team seems strong so far!"

"Hockey sounds like a fun escape from dreary winters."

Thursday, November 24, 1960: Sad

In Gloversville for Thanksgiving, I felt eager to talk to my cousins. We knew nothing about our relatives' tiny new kitten whose leash Aunt Myrna had hooked to the clothesline. Tiger could run freely on the grass and part of the driveway. We were in tears after Tiger, invisible behind the car wheels, got run over when Mom backed into the driveway. She felt awful. Before my birth, Mom liked her cat Smokey more than she likes her daughter now!

Lydia and Ella were more upset with Aunt Myrna than with Mom. Too devastated for Thanksgiving dinner, they cried in their room for hours. Feeling sad for everyone, I felt helpless to make anyone feel better. It was the worst holiday! After a quiet meal, Dad drove us home before dark. Trying to be positive, he said, "We were lucky the drive was less windy than on Thanksgiving in 1950. Albany had the strongest ever wind gust of 83 mph with sustained winds of 50 to 60 mph."

I prayed that my cousins will feel better soon and that this accident isn't a setback for Mom, still mourning for Grandma.

Friday, November 25, 1960: Post-Holiday

Dominic's dance party tonight included good hit records like *Alley Oop* and *Itsy Bitsy Teenie Weenie Yellow Polka Dot Bikini*. Jed said, "Angela, I bet you'd look great in a bikini."

My face felt hot. "Thank you, Jed."

Dancing with Jake to *The Twist*, I realized my need to practice to be smoother.

I could have slow danced all night with Dominic. With eyes closed, I felt chills hearing Ray Charles' rich voice and moving to the sexy rhythm of *Georgia on My Mind*.

A great time with Dominic and Jake temporarily erased the image of poor dead Tiger!

Saturday, November 26, 1960: Sisters

I was happy that Eva called. "Angela, it was good to see my sisters, their nice husbands, and my infant nephew and to receive early birthday gifts. My oldest sister said that her lovely light blue pullover sweater makes my greenish eyes look bluer. With new underwear from my other sister, I can throw out the tattered stuff."

I giggled. "You're lucky to have sisters!"

"I appreciate them, but I'm eight and eleven years younger and they aren't into nineteenth century literature."

I laughed. "Will you babysit for your nephew?"

"When he's less destructible. Can you believe that I'm forcing my love of Christmas glitz onto him? I couldn't resist giving him a little snow village with a tiny artificial Christmas tree." We chuckled.

"I adore the kids of my cousins Beth, Nick, and Justine… After finishing the novel *Advise and Consent,* I plan to read more books you've liked on the SAT (scholastic aptitude test) list. *Wuthering Heights* and *Pride and Prejudice* were special! I want to read other Jane Austen novels. What are you reading?"

"After completing Page 1136 of Michener's remarkable novel *Hawaii,* I'll trudge to the library for new books."

Tuesday, November 29, 1960: Weather

The high temperature of fifty-seven was a treat compared to the usual low forties. Despite a couple of inches of November snow, I've been happy walking the mile from school in warmer-than-usual temperatures! If only this weather lasts…

Thursday, December 1, 1960: Grades

After Mom signed my second report card of the year, Dad said, "Last time you got all *A*s. Why did intermediate algebra go down to *B*?"

Ill at ease, I shrugged. "I got 89 on the six-week test." Wouldn't most parents be happy with only one *B*?

Friday, December 2, 1960: The Wind

After this week's fun phone talks with Craig (over an hour), Luke, Dominic, and Jake, I flirted with Jake and Dominic at the movies tonight. Everyone was enthusiastic about *Inherit the Wind* starring Spencer Tracy, Frederic March, and dancer Gene Kelly.

Marcus, who bought me a soda and sat with us, explained: "This movie is based on the play about the 1920s trial of Scopes, a high school science teacher accused of teaching Darwin's theory of evolution, which still upsets some religious people. I read that McCarthy's 1950s witch hunt inspired the movie's support of intellectual freedom and the right to speak out."

Dominic said, "It's shameful how many lives McCarthy's accusations of communism ruined." I missed Sara, who felt angry about McCarthy and loved movies like this. I'm eager to communicate with Sara again next month!

Saturday, December 3, 1960: *Nabucco*

On the radio, Metropolitan Opera singers serenading Mom and me made housecleaning less tedious. This melodic Italian opera is based on the bible story of Babylonian King Nebuchadnezzar conquering the Jews. Our encyclopedia mentioned the secret love between a Jewish leader and the king's daughter, who converts to Judaism. I can't imagine Dominic and Jake converting. But Julia's Protestant mom and Jewish dad seem happy attending the Unitarian Church.

Friday, December 9, 1960: Jack Frost Dance

At lunch, I said, "Doreen, I'm glad that you're attending the semiformal tonight! Have a great time with JP!"

"Thank you, Angela. I can't wait to see the gym decorated with dolls, teddy bears, and rock-and-roll records hanging from the ceiling for the theme *While We're Young*! After football players receive awards, the dance king and queen will be crowned in a merry-go-round throne! I'll miss you."

"I'm crushed about missing this spectacular dance again. After heartwarming phone calls and party fun with Jake, Dominic, and Craig, I could have had a ball with any of them."

"Though I prefer Jews, I'd rather go with a gentile than miss the dance."

I hugged Doreen. "I'm glad that you understand how I feel."

Saturday, December 10, 1960: Basketball

After Dominic called, I sat with him and Jake at our game. Afterwards, Jake escorted me to the Boulevard. Loads of AHS kids stood to sing our school song, which chokes me up:

Hail alma mater, hats off to you
Ever you'll find us loyal and true
Firm and undaunted, ever we'll be
Albany High we love, here's a toast to thee!

Jake's sense of humor, brains, and marvelous person-ality made a long walk from Robin Street west on Central Avenue fun.

Tuesday, December 13, 1960: Hanukkah

I can't wait to finish college and get a good job to afford holiday and birthday presents! I'm tired of making home-made cards because I lack money to buy gifts for friends and relatives.

Wednesday, December 14, 1960: Sixteen

At Schuyler, I warmed up from tonight's frigid temperature while watching Eva in a lead role in *Christmas in the Market Place*. Afterwards, I gave her a hug and my hand-made card and sang *Happy Birthday* in a whisper because I'm off key. "Eva, I'm impressed with your acting! Did you mind working on your birthday?"

"Thank you! I had nothing better to do." We chuckled.

"You look lovely in your costume and makeup! The program says that you're secretary of the dramatics club! Congratulations!"

"I appreciate your encouragement, Angela!"

"How's your social life?"

"Parties and movies with groups of classmates and dates with a smart, musical senior in the chorus have been fun. Tony's cute and very nice."

"You deserve someone special! Happy Sweet Sixteen, Eva!"

*Play: costumed Eva, seated in front
of her friend May standing*

Thursday, December 15, 1960: Music

At the AHS orchestra concert, the full choir marched in while singing *Adeste Fideles*, whose Latin words I can translate and whose melody I like. A senior girl soloist with a lovely voice sang *I Wonder as I Wonder*. The smaller inner choir and the dozen Albanette girls sang other carols. I can't help but like most Christmas songs, despite feeling left out this time of year.

Saturday, December 24, 1960: Vacation

On the last day of school, Jake, enthusiastic about RPI's upcoming hockey tournament, walked me home. It's been dreamy to receive his almost daily phone calls and to talk on the phone to Dominic regularly for up to two hours, Luke a few times, Craig once, and Udeh once. In a colder-than-average month, last night's low was eleven below zero! After enjoying the Metropolitan Opera's comic *L'Elisir d'Amore* on the radio during housecleaning, I was happy snuggling in my room reading the excellent bestseller *Dr. Zhivago*. Russia sounds colder than Albany! Even hibernating, I find vacation freedom delightful.

Sunday, December 25, 1960: Christmas

Our Gloversville relatives came for dinner at our house. Catching up with my cousins was fun! Lydia described freshman year at Gloversville High. "It beats junior high. Since Len broke up because I wouldn't have sex, I've enjoyed older, taller, athletic boys."

"Do you miss Len?" I asked.

"I liked him but wasn't in love or crazy enough to risk pregnancy. Our Jewish gang still sees movies together. We tall girls snap fingers in front of the boys' glazed eyes on the level of our boobs to stop their staring."

I giggled. "What activities have you joined?"

Lydia grinned. "Glee club has cute Italian boys who sing well!"

"After falling for two Italian charmers, I'm sympathetic. Paul still makes my heart beat fast. My friend Eva dates an Italian who sings in her chorus. Have you danced?"

"I hear the music while working in our store until 9 PM when Gloversville's Friday dances end!"

"That's awful! Won't your parents let you attend once?" She shook her head no.

I asked, "Can you attend big dances if only gentiles invite you?"

"If anyone had asked me to the fall harvest dance, I would have gone. Dad's busy in the store. My friend Joan, who's up for any mischief, will help me get around Mom. Joan's told me all about sex, not that we've done it." We giggled.

"Though I've met amusing Craig, Dominic, and Jake at school events, I've yet to figure out how to transport a formal dress and sneak out to a dance. I've been heartbroken because my parents' stupid dating rule has made me miss four big dances. Since I had to turn down great dancer Craig, whose maternal grandmother is Jewish, a year ago, word's been out about my parents. Gentiles know I can't accept invites!"

"That's a shame! Since I tower over the eight Gloversville Jewish boys, my parents' position is weak. Could Craig have picked you up at a friend's house?"

"Protestant Eva lives too far away and attends a school with different dances. My parents might lock me in until graduation if they found out from Jewish friends' parents that I dated a gentile. You know my father's scary temper. All year, I've avoided and disliked the parents."

"Anyone would!" said Lydia.

"Though Jewish Luke calls regularly, he and the few other Jewish guys probably invite faster girls to dances." Both cousins nodded sympathetically.

Monday, December 26, 1960: St. Ann's

On the phone, I said, "Merry Christmas, Eva! How was your holiday?"

"Very nice! Tony took me to St. Ann's on Fourth Avenue for Christmas Eve Mass with his father, older sister, and younger brother. His mother was home cooking. I saw Ric and Alice with their many older siblings."

"I like Alice! Tony must be serious to introduce you to his family."

"It's okay that he avoids discussing feelings. I'm too young for anything serious."

"Most boys say so little that I'm unsure whether each date is the last." We laughed.

"Angela, are you thinking of Yeats?"

"Yes. Though I declined going steady, I said that I liked him, enjoyed our dates, and wanted to keep seeing him."

"Do you ever see him?"

"Only at Forum, the AHS current events club. Occupied as president, he ignores me."

Tuesday, December 27, 1960: Beth Emeth

At the Reformed synagogue dance, Luke and I talked all evening. At the Boulevard, Luke and his pal ordered bargain French fried onion rings and shrimp cocktails. Enjoying my yummy French fries and chocolate milk, I felt enthralled by Luke's deep voice speaking enthusiastically about Kennedy's idea of a New Frontier in space. I imagined slow dancing with him at dark, romantic Mike's Log Cabin.

Saturday, December 31, 1960: Resolution

While the parents danced at our Conservative synagogue's New Year's Eve party, I enjoyed peace and quiet reading the superb Charlotte Bronte novel *Jane Eyre*. My 1961 resolution is to dump my *Brain* image. It's unfair that cool, smart Jewish boys ask out only pretty girls with lower grades! How do I keep my grades and have a good social life with dates for school dances with un-boring Jews? Next New Year's Eve, I want to be out dancing with a boy I like romantically.

Parents at party

1961 AHS Junior

Beware of monotony; it's the mother of all the deadly sins.
Edith Wharton

Monday, January 2, 1961: Ritual

Eva called to say, "Happy 1961! Except for yesterday's nine inches of snow, is anything new?"

"Yesterday, Jake took me to my first Catholic Mass!"

"How did it compare to Dominic's Greek Orthodox service?"

"Able to translate Latin, but not Greek, prayers, I gave a point to the Mass. The more ornate pageantry of the Greeks won them a point. After years of repetitive synagogue services, any novel religious experience is special."

"How was Jake?"

"Like Craig and Dominic, he's fun, gentlemanly, and smart. After Mass, Jake quipped, 'Are you ready to convert?' We chuckled after I replied, 'Sure! When my parents say yes.'"

"How was his family?"

"His friendly parents, younger brother, pretty older sister, Jake, and I played Scrabble, canasta, and darts. His kind, smart mom, who is stocky like Jake, made me feel welcome. During a tasty dinner, his trim dad described in amusing detail RPI's hockey tournament victory over Harvard, New Brunswick, and Princeton. While the Rose Parade played on TV, Jake and I went to the basement where he sang with the record. "Santa, if you will use your magic, this

Christmas Eve while I'm holding her tight, then we'll whisper the proper things and wear each other's ring."

Eva sang, "Santa, make her my bride for Christmas."

"I love *Christmas Bride* and felt elated after Jake kissed me twice on the lips."

"How about Dominic and Craig?"

"I'm wild about the Latin class triumvirate! The Jack Frost would have been dreamy with any of them...or all three." We laughed.

Tuesday, January 3, 1961: Married Twenty-Four Years

With a Pillsbury yellow cake mix, I made my parents an anniversary cake. Though Dad's sweet tooth produced wholehearted thanks, Mom complained. "I'm avoiding fattening desserts to lose weight."

Saturday, January 7, 1961: My Sixteenth

After Jake and his mom brought nice birthday cards, Dad asked, "Angela, can you help me shop for a tie?" Though the request seemed odd, I nodded yes and welcomed a rare chance to be with Dad without domineering Mom.

Home from Central Avenue around six, we entered the foyer and heard assorted voices say, "Surprise! Happy Sweet Sixteenth Birthday!" With seven party guests, I went to the Center where I danced mainly with Marcus and his cousin before returning to my house. A party was unexpected because Dad earns nothing and Mom's promotion is still pending. Appreciating the party, I tried to be good company with boys my parents chose. I thanked them for the party, corsage, perfume, and gold *16* bracelet charm!

"Being surprised was fun! Dad, your Uncle Sam generously sent sixteen dollars!"

"My uncle's the life of the party," commented Dad, who has joked less since losing his job.

Sunday, January 8, 1961: Silent Wrath

Mom asked, "Angela, did you like the party guests?"

"Doreen, Marsha, and Tara were great!"

Mom inquired, "How about Jed, prior dates Marcus and Phil, and Marcus' cousin?"

"I look forward to reading Marcus' book gifts: Beatnik poetry and quantum physics!"

Mom persisted. "How about the boys?"

My best, honest answer was, "They're nice."

"Whom do you prefer?" Mom sounded annoyed.

"I have fun with Luke, Craig, Jake, and Dominic."

Dad hollered, "Only Luke is Jewish! For crying out loud, forget those non-Jewish boys!"

I bit my tongue to avoid voicing these thoughts:

Stop shouting at me for honestly answering your question! I can't wait to escape from your childish tantrums and narrow minds! Forcing Jews on me is useless. In college, I'll date anyone I want, including Negroes! I'll always remember how you meanly ruined my AHS social life!

Exasperated, I left to write thank-you notes for lovely presents, including a scent atomizer and Marsha's stuffed autograph giraffe. Radio hits like the Shirelles' *Will You Love Me Tomorrow* improved my mood.

Monday, January 9, 1961: Pearls

Along with a birthday card to Marsha who'll turn sweet six-teen on Wednesday, I mailed this:

> Dear Aunt Lila, Uncle Bert, Hal, and Ron,
> Thank you so much for my favorite sweet-sixteen gift, the fantabulous necklace of sixty-seven cultured pearls! The twenty-inch length and slight size gradation are ideal for my outfits! I really like the pale cream color and white gold clasp. The elegant red alligator case with cream satin lining beautifully protects my favorite necklace! I plan to wear this generous gift on every possible occasion for the rest of my life! I love it! Thanks again for the perfect present!
> Love, Angela

Thursday, January 12, 1961: Mom's Birthday

Without enough allowance for a gift and discouraged from baking a cake, I made my usual birthday card with some artwork. After Dad takes Mom and me to Jack's Famous Restaurant on lower State Street Sunday, I'll be hibernating while studying for mid-years.

Friday, January 20, 1961: Inauguration

What a great day for our country! Kennedy is president! Despite a huge snow storm, Jackie Kennedy looked chic in a beige wool coat with matching large covered buttons. She must have frozen with only a small fur collar and round hat perched on her head. A muff warmed her hands. Kennedy's speech was stirring! On the phone, Jake, as enthusiastic as I, quoted the best lines:

> Man holds in his mortal hands the power to abolish all forms of human poverty and all forms of human life.
>
> If a free society cannot help the many who are poor, it cannot save the few who are rich.
>
> United there is little we cannot do in a host of cooperative ventures. Divided there is little we can do.
>
> In the long history of the world, only a few generations have been granted the role of defending freedom in its hour of maximum danger.
>
> Let us never negotiate out of fear. But let us never fear to negotiate.
>
> (We must) bear the burden of a long twilight struggle...against the common enemies of man: tyranny, poverty, disease, and war itself.
>
> Ask not what your country can do for you, ask what you can do for your country.

Jake continued, "His *chiasmus* in the last line is beautiful!"

"Thanks to Latin, I recognize it."

"Kennedy too probably translated Cicero's speeches, including this notable *chiasmus: "flebat uterque non de suo supplicio, sed pater de filii morte, de patris filius."*

"Does that mean, 'Each wept, not for his own punishment or humiliation, but the father for the death of the son, the son for the death of his father'?"

"Yes! It's very moving. Angela, we have an educated man of culture leading us! Inviting Robert Frost to read one of his poems was ideal!"

"Jake, does Nixon even know what a poem is?" He chuckled before we hung up to study for exams.

Sunday, January 29, 1961: Travell

I knew that things would improve with Kennedy in charge! His appointment of Janet Travell, MD, the first woman to be a President's official doctor, is gratifying!

Tuesday, January 31, 1961: Ursa

Forum reelected President Yeats, who still attracts me, and Secretary Angela, the hibernating *Ursa* (Latin for she-bear). Bears are smart to snuggle in their dens during months like this with daily highs of fifteen or twenty degrees. Only phone calls from Jake almost daily, Dominic regularly, and Luke, Craig, and Udeh occasionally relieved the monotony of chores and exam preparation. I'm relieved and thankful to get these grades: intermediate algebra and Spanish 96, Latin 97, English 98, and American history 99.

Wednesday, February 1, 1961: Chimp

At lunch, Jake said, "Did you hear that we launched into space chimpanzee Ham for over sixteen minutes and returned him unharmed, except for a bruised nose?"

After we chuckled, Dominic lamented, "We're still behind the Russians."

Craig remarked, "Though their dog-onauts came back safely last summer, our astro-chimp is closer to a human and performed a task while in space."

Laughing at the names, I asked, "What task?"

Jake replied, "Ham pushed a lever almost as quickly as on earth."

After we chortled, Dominic revealed, "I'd love to be an astronaut!"

Craig commented, "I'd rather not die young. How about you, Angela?"

I joked, "I'll go only with one of you. If we don't return, at least I'll die laughing."

Thursday, February 2, 1961: Lee

I'm pleased that Latin Club President Jake will lead the meetings and do the work while I loaf as veep. I'm glad that Julia, whose birthday is soon, won secretary and that personable Lee is treasurer. With an excellent build, sexy smile, and smooth cocoa-colored skin, Lee participates in football, wrestling, and track. His magnetism reminds me of Paul, but Lee seems more easygoing. When we smile at each other, I wonder whether he'd like to date me. I'm sad that even at AHS, where smart Negro kids are usually popular and elected to office, no white kids date them. If my parents knew about my yen for Lee, they'd have a conniption.

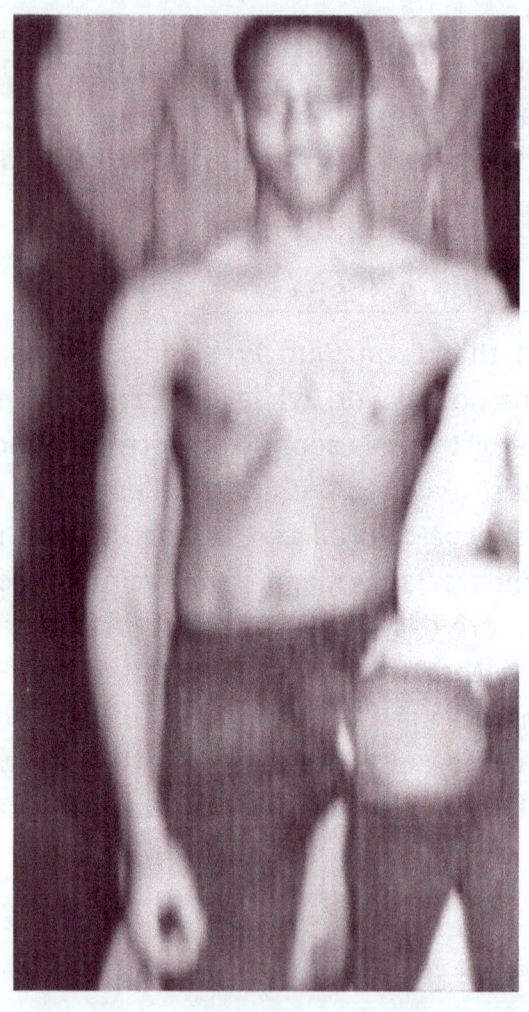

Wrestler Lee

Friday, February 3, 1961: Cold

No wonder we're in the doldrums after January temperatures as low as seventeen below zero and over seventeen inches of snow. The average minimum temperature was worse than usual at only six degrees above zero!

Down about Sara's continued silence, I can't ask Mom without revealing that I secretly read Sara's note.

Hearing about Patroon School classmate G, I felt a cold dread about how easily girls' futures are ruined. Sweet but un-bright G trusted her careless boyfriend, who disappeared after her pregnancy got her expelled from AHS.

Sunday, February 5, 1961: Zero

Mom said, "Lila reported that the NYC area has had over twenty inches of snow!"

Reading the newspaper, Dad said, "Yesterday, our low temperature was finally higher than zero after an all-time record of fifteen straight below-zero nights and some daytime temperatures below zero!"

Mom added, "Myrna called about the three feet of Gloversville snow they're shoveling...we're lucky our old oil furnace is working." Which is worse: bitter cold with wind or tons of snow? It's just as well that I must study. Walking home from school is enough time outdoors. Our neighbor kindly drops his daughter and me at AHS when he works in town.

Tuesday, February 7, 1961: Storm

The frightening blizzard, which has killed at least seventy people and dropped up to forty inches of snow in central NYS, has made it too dangerous for Dad, after dropping Mom at work, to drive around trying to sell door-to-door. Although he never gives up, he must feel terrible without income for over a year. Dad's job woes scare me into doing my best in school. With a college degree, Dad might have a secure job which pays well.

Thursday, February 9, 1961: Frightful Nightmare

I dreamt that Doreen and I, on a double date, attended a sorority dance in below-zero weather. Her date, a college man, drove us to Emmy's Brauhaus in the Helderberg Mountains. On the way home, it was snowing hard. The car skidded into a snow bank, stranding us without houses nearby. I woke myself before discovering whether we froze to death. I can't wait for milder winters after leaving Albany.

Tuesday, February 14, 1961: Valentine

I was pleasantly surprised to receive a little valentine with a bear holding a heart from a sophomore (four months younger) in my Spanish II class. Though Jim sometimes walks me home, I can't take seriously an un-dateable Protestant flirt, even though he is smart and outgoing and makes me laugh. Knowing about my soft spot for bears, he signed the valentine *Su Osito*. This pet Spanish name he gave himself means *your little male bear*. I laughed at the addressee: *Osa Mamacita*, which he said means *beautiful female bear*, rather than the literal *little mother bear*.

Thursday, February 16, 1961: Boys' and Girls' Night

I ventured out on a snowy, freezing evening for the annual competition of the four AHS literary societies. *Culture*, the girls' one-act comedy, was humorous. The boys debated whether the Federal government should substantially increase Federal aid to secondary education in the United States. Since my favorite boys are in Philalogia, I regretted Udeh, Lon, and Neal losing to Philadoxia seniors. After the serious and humorous declamations, other junior girls presented the prophecy of the seniors' futures.

Friday, February 17, 1961: Tragedy

I'm in shock that a Belgian plane crash has killed the entire American team of eighteen figure skaters and nine coaches and officials en route to the World Championships in Prague! It's so sad! At least Olympic gold winners Heiss and Jenkins survived because they were not competing!

Monday, February 20, 1961: Don't Hold Your Breath

Mom reported, "I thanked Mr. McAllister for another follow-up with Personnel. The job analysis and most approvals for my upgrade are completed. The director should sign off within two weeks. Mr. McAllister said, 'Fern, you certainly deserve to be a Senior Typist.'"

I thought: you certainly don't deserve to win mother of the year!

Dad thanked her for the good news.

Tuesday, February 21, 1961: Feast or Famine

After smart senior Jerry was the second boy to invite me to the Blue Moon formal dance, Doreen and I chuckled about two invitations after none for fourteen months. She asked, "Which invite's better?"

I giggled. "Luke, Craig, Dominic, or Jake...seriously, I'm glad that Marcus asked first."

Later, I sang words from an Elvis hit. "Are you lonesome tonight...tell me, dear, are you lonesome tonight?"

Sunday, February 26, 1961: Curie

I called Eva to rave about a biography I just finished, *Madame Curie*! "What an inspiring role model! Overcoming obstacles as a woman scientist, she married a loving husband, raised two talented daughters, and won Nobel Prizes in physics and chemistry!"

"Thanks for the tip! I'll look for it at the library!"

Tuesday, February 28, 1961: Game

I enjoyed a phone chat with Luke, who has called more lately. At our basketball game, I was happy that Jake sat with me! Today's above-freezing temperature lightened our moods. After forty-seven inches of depressing snow this winter, we long for early spring weather.

Thursday, March 2, 1961: Peace Corps

Dominic sounded excited about our beloved President Kennedy's new Peace Corps. "Ten years ago as a Congressman, Kennedy first suggested the idea in a speech. I'd love to volunteer."

I responded, "Dominic, it's wonderful that Americans will be able to travel overseas to help people in developing countries and to show that some of us aren't *Ugly Americans*."

Friday, March 3, 1961: Eva's

At Eva's party, I was happy to hear her whisper, "Xavier and Ric are talking to me again."

"What changed?" I murmured.

Eva grinned. "Without explanation, they began talking as if nothing had occurred. Xavier looks better, has more friends, and seems happy with Paul's ex. Ric has the role of my mate in *George Washington Slept Here*."

"Do you kiss him?" I giggled.

She smiled. "I hope so."

After a perfect evening of dancing, flirting, and laughing with the Latin class triumvirate, I thanked Eva. "I had a ball at your fabulous party!"

Saturday, March 4, 1961: Blue Moon

I felt lucky when Marcus arrived with a lovely corsage of white rose buds for my wrist. His eyes seemed to widen, as if he hardly recognized me, but he didn't compliment my appearance.

Mom, president of Marcus' fan club, was in a tizzy seeing him look his best in a dark suit. Saying, "Let's use up this roll of film for quick processing," Mom made us pose for so many photos that we almost missed the dance.

At the dance, Doreen said, "I love your hair teased in a beehive and your new strapless, ballerina-length, turquoise organza! You look elegant, the best ever!"

"Thank you! I was lucky to find this bargain dress! You look beautiful! Coral pink complements your auburn hair!"

Afterwards, Mom asked, "How was it?"

"The theme was *Heavenly*. The Milky Way covered one wall. I loved seeing all the kids dressed up and looking great! Marcus and I mingled and danced to the music of the Siena College Collegians. At Herbert's with two couples, we danced." Because Mom practically has me married off to Marcus, I omitted that it was better than expected.

At my best

Sunday, March 5, 1961: Recap

When Eva called about the dance, I reported, "I hardly rec-ognized the gym with a ceiling of glittery silver stars which resembled diamonds sparkling!"

"How was Marcus?"

"Better than at school when he and his cousin make asides and snigger, like eight-year-olds in tall bodies. Eva, am I wrong about their secret jokes ridiculing others?"

"I have the impression that they look down on less smart classmates. Was his cousin there?"

"No. Marcus was a gentleman. We danced a lot and I had as good a time as possible with a boy I like platonically."

"Is your mother happy?"

"After enjoying the Blue Moon more than I, she has secretly ordered engagement announcements." We giggled.

"Would you accept more dates with Marcus?"

"Why not? Aside from wonderful phone calls from Craig, Jake, Dominic, and Luke, my social life is comatose. How are you?"

"Extracurricular activities counteract academic bore-dom. Chorus and dramatics, which require substantial rehearsal time, create the illusion of being artistic." She snickered at herself.

"Eva, you are artistic! I'm waving my magic wand to send you a male genius with a great sense of humor, a *rara avis*. How's Paul?"

"Irresistible." Eva laughed.

"I hope that he shows interest in you as an increasingly glamorous and beautiful actress."

"Thank you but who wants to be in a harem of hundreds?" We tittered.

"How's Xavier?"

"Though he calls some evenings, baseball practice, the school newspaper, science society, Key Club, and his girlfriend leave him little time to chat."

"Eva, I miss you and wish I could see you at AHS."

Friday, March 10, 1961: Birthday

I felt sorry for poor Dad, turning fifty after seven inches of snow fell and the high temperature was twenty-four degrees. He got thrilling presents like underwear and socks. The *Happy Birthday* song was more a punishment than a gift because Mom and I sing off key. After the steak dinner Mom and I made, Dad blew out all fifty birthday candles. Enjoying our attention, he cracked jokes about being old enough for a rocking chair.

Our darling parakeet, almost seven years old, came through by including I Love You and Happy Birthday among the gibberish of his evening oration. Tumba seems to sense occasions when these special presents are needed. Of course, we make a big fuss to reward him. I can't help laughing when he repeats, "Tumba is a good boy!"

Sunday, March 12, 1961: Oh No

Dad said, "For better family relationships, we made a low-cost appointment with a social worker at the Jewish Family Service on South Lake Avenue. Meet us there Wednesday after I pick up Mom at work."

Raising my eyebrows in surprise, I was speechless. Has my cold war with the parents caused this latest bombshell? Will we see the 1960 therapist who got Sara's letter, which the parents don't know I've secretly read?

Tuesday, March 14, 1961: Escapes

AHS's orchestra concert included Handel's *Water Music, Holiday for Trombones, Girl in Satin,* and *Flower Drum Song* selections. After I complimented Dominic's violin playing, he replied, "Though I love solo piano, making music as part of a group is a joy!"

"Doesn't practice take too much time away from homework?"

He chuckled. "Music's more fun. My next escape from homework is track and cross country running."

I laughed. "Are you still in dramatics?"

"Yes. I enjoy Forum and Latin Club with you, Angela." He blushed. Our eyes met as we both beamed. Appreciating his cheek dimples, I imagined the gentle touch of his musical fingers.

"Dominic, those are fun, as well as our literary societies. Next year, I'll take a lighter course load to have more time for activities."

He bantered, "Tell me which activities to join to be with you."

I felt a blush. "Nothing on stage! I'm the opposite of an extravert like you, Dominic!"

Wednesday, March 15, 1961: Social Work

Nearing the Family Service building, I laughed at myself, skulking around so that no one I know saw me. Expecting a Jewish woman, I wondered whether Dominic knows our Greek-named social worker, a brunette with a wedding ring. Less overweight and slightly younger than my parents, he wore glasses.

In a small, plain beige office, we three sat in front of Mr. V's brown wooden desk. Dad's description of his job loss, Sara's attack and departure, and Grandma's death suggested that Mr. V is new to my parents.

I felt on the defensive while Mom complained. "Angela spends all her time with friends. Why invest our time, energy, money, and love into raising a girl we never see?"

Dad added, "If Angela goes away to college, she'll be here only another year."

After Mr. V inquired, "You want to spend time with your daughter before she leaves home?" the parents nodded.

When Mr. V looked at me, I answered: "You see me every night at dinner and during my many hours cooking, washing dishes, and vacuuming the house. Most evenings, I'm home doing schoolwork. In my little free time, I need fun with friends who like me."

After Mr. V asked, "Does that mean that you feel unloved at home?" I nodded yes. He asked, "Can you say more?"

"Despite all my housework and report cards with mainly As, I'm called a 'bad daughter,' and forbidden to date the best boys at school. After making Mom gifts, like a hand-knitted muffler in her favorite color, I've heard, 'I don't want your presents. All I need is a good daughter.' Everyone avoids people who continually criticize and unfairly punish them."

"Thanks for sharing that…Our time is up for today."

Tired of parental criticism, I was relieved that Mr. V arranged individual sessions. To avoid being stigmatized as having psychological problems, I'll keep counseling a secret. Uncle Jules misunderstood artistic Sara enough to have her committed to a locked mental hospital. I missed her today. She seemed saner and wiser than my parents and other adults.

Monday, March 20, 1961: Report Card

I was relieved to get *As*, except a *B* in trigonometry, which replaced intermediate algebra. Dad signed the card without comment about the *B*. Is he used to my careless math errors?

Thursday, March 23, 1961: Meet Me

Dominic said, "Meet me at *Meet Me in St. Louis!*" Elated to sit with the Latin class triumvirate at this school musical, I enjoyed songs like *The Boy Next Door, The Trolley Song,* and *Have Yourself a Merry Little Christmas.*

AHS band and orchestra bass player Bob walked me to the Boulevard. He held my hand, had his arm around me, and kissed me on the cheek. A slightly younger, forbidden Protestant sophomore, he has dark blond hair sleeked back into a duck tail and blue eyes. He's nice but the triumvirate are smarter and funnier.

Friday, March 24, 1961: Hospital

I felt concerned when Jake said, "My mother's hospitalized for a routine operation."

"I'm sorry that she has to go through that. Your mom's special! Is she feeling up to visitors outside the family?"

"Your visit will speed her recovery. She likes you." At the hospital, Jake held my hand and had his arm around me. His sweet mother looked cheerier after seeing us and reading the get-well card I made from pink and purple colored paper.

Saturday, March 25, 1961: Ancient Rome

Three brainy, personable sophs and juniors Craig, Jake, and I were Mrs. G's team at the Baird Latin Contest at NY University's Washington Square College of Arts and Science! On the train to NYC, I was happy that Craig sat with me and held my hand. After the contest and lunch, I enjoyed being with him on the bus uptown and at the movie. Everyone liked *Spartacus*, starring Rex's uncle Kirk Douglas, famous Laurence Olivier, Peter Ustinov, Tony Curtis, and Jean Simmons. Barred from dating my favorite boys, I related to the slaves fighting Julius Caesar and other ancient Romans for freedom. The action-packed movie was ideal for Latin students who have read Caesar's *Gallic Wars*. Jake said, "I read that JFK courageously helped end blacklisting of writers by crossing an American Legion picket line to see this movie."

I answered, "I love Kennedy! He gives me hope for the future of our country."

On the train home, Craig cracked us up by periodically standing up, beating on his slim chest, and announcing, "I am Spartacus!" What a marvelous, tremendous, terrific day! I had an absolute blast!

Tuesday, March 28, 1961: Warm

Though the average high this time of year is forty-nine, today's high of seventy-three degrees was exhilarating. Walking home from school, I was grinning for no reason. The May and June proms popped into my head. On the phone, I told Doreen, "After missing the 1960 junior and senior proms, I've changed my old dream wheel to a *dance wheel* with Jewish boys' names. At bedtime, I'll spin to choose a boy and send him a telepathic message to dream about me and ask me to his prom."

"Who are the boys?"

"Yeats, Luke, Lon, Hank, Rex, and Zeke are the best. For the dozen needed, I added Victor, Artie, Phil, Frankie, Marcus, and Myles."

"I hope it works, Angela!" We giggled at the sheer fun of it.

Wednesday, March 29, 1961: Outraged

After I sneaked into Mr. V's office undetected, he asked, "What changes would make you happier?"

"Different parents!" I jested. After he smiled, I continued. "I'd respect them if they apologized for ruining my social life for sixteen months and let me date gentiles again. For the first of only two formal school dances for sophomores, turning down great dancer Craig, a smart leader with a Jewish maternal grandmother, broke my heart! Mom said, 'Act nice and a Jewish boy will ask you.' For years, I've flirted with Jewish Hank and Lon, who treat me as a pal. I missed both dances. This year, I again missed the Jack Frost when I could have had a ball with special boys like Craig, Jake, or Dominic!"

"How did you feel?"

"Outraged to be punished with the same rule, like a delinquent whose privileges are taken away for years. I'm upset that the respectful boys I'm most comfortable with are banned. I can only talk to them on the phone and at school events."

"How do you feel about your parents?"

"I dislike hypocrites who should practice what they preach about bigoted behavior being wrong. After emphasizing that Negroes and Jews deserve equal treatment, they discriminate against Christians! My mother, who was asked out only after high school, has seemed envious that I've had boyfriends since junior high."

"You'd like to respect your parents. You want the dating rule changed to feel loved and be treated fairly?" After I nodded yes, he added, "They expressed concern that dating gentiles might lead to marrying out of your religion."

"I'm only sixteen. I want to dance, laugh, and go on fun dates without getting serious until after college."

"Have you dated Jewish boys?"

"Last spring, Yeats was fun. Though I invited him to my sorority formal, I got no invite to his junior prom. When he later asked to go steady, I responded, 'I really like you and have fun on our dates. I'm too young to go steady but I want to keep dating you.' I was hurt and disappointed that he stopped asking me out.

"In February, I felt lucky when Marcus invited me to our formal dance. I tried to be a good date, but we had little in common and conversation was an effort. Though open to another date, I wasn't sorry when he didn't ask." I laughed. "My mother has a crush on him and wants him as a son-in-law."

He smiled. "Any other Jewish boys?"

"I like good conversationalists who read; Jed annoyed me, trying to make out in public and watching TV on dates. Luke invited me to a 1959 dance. After I had to turn down unchaperoned party invitations from him and another Jewish boy I like, they stopped inviting me out. We girls must wait for boys to ask. My parents don't realize that the few intelligent, personable Jewish boys avoid dating goody-goodies whose parents require party chaperones and who want to stay virgins until marriage. The few attractive Jewish guys pressure girls to go farther than the Christians I prefer."

"Is a girl's virginity public knowledge?"

I tittered. "We wear circle pins on the left, rather than right, lapels to advertise it."

Mr. V smiled. "I appreciate your sharing. You can live with your parents' rules if you are free to date gentiles?" Nodding, I felt comfortable with nice Mr. V who seemed neutral and wisely avoided siding with the enemy adults.

Sunday, April 2, 1961: NYC

Visiting our relatives with my parents, I was happy to receive a phone call from Donald! I asked, "How do you like Queens College?"

"Better than high school...British literature, social sciences, and classical music appreciation are my favorites. Then there's calculus and physiology." We laughed.

Tuesday, April 11, 1961: Snow

Sophomore Bob continues to chase me with phone calls and hand-holding while walking me home. Today, we waded through almost six inches of depressing snow!

At dinner, Dad said, "After five years in the hick town Northville before you were born, Albany winters with less snow and warmer temperatures seem moderate."

Wednesday, April 12, 1961: Religion

Mr. V mentioned the parents' concern because I seem uninterested in Judaism and avoid the synagogue.

I snickered. "Their rigid dating rule makes Judaism seem segregationist and punitive. I appreciate getting out of services with repetitious boring Hebrew prayers. Only Frankie's father's sermons interest me. I used to attend to flirt, but my current crushes attend other synagogues or aren't Jewish."

"Any other thoughts?"

"Since age five, I've resented males getting the good seats downstairs in orthodox synagogues. Females are as smart and good as males and should be rabbis and cantors. If women can't have multiple husbands, why should biblical men like Abraham have more than one wife? Females should have been treated as equals in the Bible, which should no longer be used by any religion."

"Any other reasons you've lost interest in Judaism?"

"I need to respect the leaders as the best people, rather than rich businessmen who aren't always honest or caring. In NYC, women sitting in the bad balcony seats disrespectfully talked through the whole service, usually about material things. Maybe they were retaliating for being treated as second-class citizens. I think they should pay attention or stay home. I believe in God and pray at bedtime."

"I appreciate your sharing your views." To avoid offending and hurting Jewish friends, I usually say nothing. Too much anti-Semitism exists for me to criticize Judaism to most Christians, whose religions should also treat females better. I spoke freely because Mr. V, working only with Jews, is like an honorary member of the tribe.

Thursday, April 13, 1961: Choir

Shouldn't religion be kept out of public schools? At the AHS choir concert, the religious songs *Great and Glorious*, *Elijah Rock*, and *There Is a Balm in Gilead* bothered me. I avoided possible conflict by keeping silent while sitting with gentlemanly Jake, my escort to the Boulevard afterwards. Enjoying hand-holding and Jake's arm around me on our Central Avenue walk, I laughed often at his jokes.

Friday, April 14, 1961: Yuri

At lunch, Jake asked, "What do you think about the Russian Yuri Gagarin orbiting earth?"

"With kids like me afraid to take science, I wonder whether America will ever catch up. How's physics?"

"Tough."

"I'm glad I'm taking Spanish. Will you be an astronaut when you grow up?" I jested.

I laughed at his reply. "If I ever grow up…don't hold your breath until I lose enough blubber to be accepted."

Saturday, April 15, 1961: Bad

On the phone, Eva shared, "After rehearsing all week, we kids from dramatics unwound at my house last night."

"Was there dancing?"

"We mainly talked. Xavier, inebriated from the beer I served, criticized me in a loud, hostile voice for being tipsy and acting phony when drunk."

"He's the pot calling the kettle black!"

"It's pure psychological projection. Because my blood sugar felt off, I was sober without my usual tiny sips of beer. He mistook diabetic wooziness for intoxication. I was relieved when his girlfriend shushed him with a *Down Boy* gesture and led him away."

I commented, "His ignoring you for over a year must have seemed better."

After agreeing with a chuckle, Eva continued. "Rather than be rude to a guest, I avoided him until the party ended. Shortly after everyone left, Ric rapped on my basement entrance. Xavier had run off after knocking down his girl-friend, who was bruised and upset. We bandaged her cut. When she was in the bathroom, Ric said, 'Xavier got mad because she took your side. I'll get her home safely.' I shook my head and rolled my eyes."

"Eva, Xavier's nastiness to you and her is shocking!"

"If she has any sense, she'll break up with him!"

"I was stupid to keep dating Mitch after he ridiculed my jacket repeatedly and dragged me along making me trip, fall, ruin my good slacks, and cut my knee.

"Did he have redeeming qualities?"

"He was a great dancer who apologized, expressed his feelings openly, and discussed the relationship. But he didn't read books or get good grades."

Tuesday, April 18, 1961: Centennial

Wonderful Mrs. E chose me to represent AHS in the NYS Civil War Centennial Commission eleven-county student honor corps! At the first statewide assembly, I got to see Darlene, a third-grade Colonie friend who represented her school. When our teacher asked me to report to American history class, I was relieved to have written this *just in case*:

> Yesterday at the Capitol, a wreath was laid at the statue of NY Civil War General Philip Sheridan. His cavalry defeated Confederate forces in Virginia's Shenandoah Valley. In 1865, Sheridan helped force General Robert E. Lee to surrender at Appomattox. Ending the war saved American lives on both sides.
>
> At Chancellors Hall on Washington Avenue, NY National Guardsmen wearing Civil War uniforms marched in and held flags during speeches to an audience of hundreds.
>
> I admired the remarks of Commission Vice President Dr. John Hope Franklin, the well-known Negro chairman of the Brooklyn College history department: "We can best observe the centennial of the Civil War by redoubling our efforts to complete the

task begun by those who fought and died to preserve the Union, eradicate the barbarism of slavery, and establish equal rights for all people."

I liked Pulitzer-Prize-winning Commission President Bruce Catton's comments: "The Civil War was about something. It was fought for something. And let us never for a moment forget it won something... the war was fought for freedom." I was excited to shake his hand while receiving the certificate he had signed.

We forty-two honor corps students had fun guiding people around the Civil War memorabilia exhibits, including President Lincoln's Emancipation Proclamation, owned by NYS. Using our handout, we students answered visitor questions. A man asked, "Were any battles fought in NYS?"

I answered, "No, but we provided more soldiers than other Northern states."

Another honor corps student mentioned a recent controversy concerning the national assembly of state centennial commissions. Host state South Carolina barred a Negro commission member from New Jersey (NJ) from eating or sleeping in the assembly hotel. NJ, NY, and other states threatened a boycott. I'm delighted that historian Catton stated, "Bigotry does not belong in any Civil War centennial meeting."

I'm glad that President Kennedy moved the meeting to the desegregated Charleston Naval Base. I'm proud that our NYS Commission is doing everything possible to "emphasize the fact that the Civil War marked America's complete dedication to the ideal of an all-embracing freedom and equality for all Americans forever." NYS's "inspired, yet tasteful and scholarly, approach" to the centennial emphasizes the reasons behind the Civil War, including current concerns, rather than "military glories."

My classmates' applause startled and pleased me.

Sunday, April 23, 1961: Zero

On the phone, I remarked, "Doreen, I've hit bottom with zero dates for almost two months."

I giggled at her reply. "I'm a desert nomad parched with thirst. I need a dating oasis!"

"You and JP are over?"

"He stopped asking me out after we drifted apart, maybe because neither of us deepened our conversations and relationship."

"I'm wondering whether JP pushed to make out more than you wanted."

"Most boys want to be physical, but I appreciated JP's acting like a gentleman and accepting limits without pressuring me. I'd be surprised if he moved on because we didn't go farther. Are you spinning the *dance wheel*?"

"For our junior prom! Happy that Luke has called often, I've held my breath only seventeen months while hoping for another date." We giggled. "Without dancing for ages, I've accepted Jed's invite to the Milne School semiformal."

"How about Jed for our prom?"

"I want to avoid hurting his feelings by encouraging him...he might try to neck again."

"At the last minute when I'm sure I won't be asked to the prom, I may invite the senior Ty."

"He's better than staying home...the junior prom with Jake would be wonderful! Last Saturday, our three-hour phone talk set a new world record, surpassing marathon talks with Dominic. After yesterday's Eastern Zone Latin Teachers' Association contest, I had a ball with Jake."

Monday, April 24, 1961: Invite

After inviting me to her school play, Eva asked about my news. I shared, "Sophomore Bob often calls and walks me home. Yesterday, he came by my house to talk."

"How do you feel about him?"

"I like that he's musical, confident, persistent about chasing me, and fun. If I could date gentiles, I'd have a better time with the brainier Latin class triumvirate. I have to admit that Bob kisses really well."

I giggled after Eva quipped, "I've yet to meet anyone I can say that about."

Wednesday, April 26, 1961: Faults

I'm okay seeing Mr. V because he encourages me to spout out opinions. When he asked what I'd like changed about my parents, I chortled. He asked, "Can you say why you laughed?"

"The word *everything* came to mind."

He smiled. "Let's start with your mother."

"She works hard. I appreciate that she buys me clothes during sales. Could competitiveness be why she has ruined my social life? Like a broken record, she repeats, 'I want to be treated with dignity and respect.' She must earn my respect by acting better and letting me date gentiles."

"Is there a recent example?"

"On Student Day, I felt lucky to win the Elmira College fourteen-karat gold key. The certificate read: The AHS faculty voted Angela Weiss the outstanding girl in the junior class in recognition of high scholastic achievement, leadership, good citizenship, and participation in extracurricular activities. Looking envious, Mom said nothing. If teachers and friends appreciate me as a nice honor student who avoids getting in trouble, don't I deserve positive words from her? Without me, she'd have to clean the house, cook dinner, and wash dishes after working full time. Most kids would complain about a broken TV. It's comical when friends' parents comment, 'Your parents must be proud to have a daughter like you.'"

"You want to date anyone you like and to feel appreciated by your mother?" I nodded yes. "How about your father?"

"At least Dad said, 'That's quite an honor!' about the award. But he must let me date boys I prefer and stop bawling me out. How can I respect a man who loses his temper like a two-year-old? When I'm on my own, I'll never put up with anyone yelling at me."

"How do you feel when your father shouts at you?"

"Trapped! Infuriated!"

Mr. V is good to listen without trying to change my mind.

Friday, April 28, 1961: Schuyler

After Bob came downtown with me, I went to the Schuyler comedy *George Washington Slept Here*. Craig, who sat with me, and I enjoyed watching Eva, looking beautiful in stage makeup, convincingly play the role of actress Rena! In the girls' room, I said, "Eva, you stole the show! Congratulations! Please sign my program."

"Thank you! It was fun." After signing, she smiled. "What did you think of Ric as Clayton, my straying husband?"

I giggled. "Looking handsome, he convinced me. I'm sorry Ric hurt your feelings by ignoring you for a year!"

"It broke my heart. During sophomore year, I really liked Ric. But he wouldn't cross Xavier."

When we joined Craig and Paul, I said, "Schuyler plays seem even better than ours at AHS. Are your kids more talented?"

Eva chuckled. "Thank you. Our sophisticated, flamboyant drama teacher, whose misaligned eye probably ruined her chances as a NYC actress, keeps us laughing. When kids misbehave or forget lines, she wisecracks about tranquilizers, 'Miltown time!'"

Grinning, I said, "Eva, you look glamorous! Are you going to a cast party?" Beaming, she nodded while Paul eyed her approvingly. I added, "You'll be the belle of the ball!"

Saturday, April 29, 1961: Kissing

Along with dancing and reading novels, kissing is one of my favorite things in life! Bob, who continues to walk me home, came by today. After we sat and talked on the back steps, I enjoyed his goodbye kisses. During phone talks some evenings with Luke, I imagine the junior prom with him including good-night kissing.

Thursday, May 4, 1961: Band

After Bob walked me home and Luke called, I attended the excellent AHS band concert. Bob and the other ninety band members looked spiffy in new uniforms: light gray jackets with garnet lapels and garnet trousers or skirts. Over pizza at the Moon, I responded to Bob's question about the concert, "I most enjoyed *The Sound of Music* medley and also liked Sousa's *Stars and Stripes Forever*. *Hendrik Hudson* was new to me."

"We played the second of Ferde Grofe's 1955 *Hudson River Suite* parts. *The River, Hendrik Hudson, Rip Van Winkle, Albany Night Boat,* and *New York* are based on Washington Irving stories. Grofe is a big band jazz player who taught at Julliard. He is famous for composing *Grand Canyon Suite* and is still alive in California." On the way home in a cab, Bob kissed my face. After a few good-night kisses, I felt euphoric.

Did Sara know Grofe at Julliard? Mom once said, "Though Sara was there from 1934 to 1939, she changed her major so much that she didn't officially graduate."

Friday, May 5, 1961: Honored

After Bob shopped with me downtown, we chatted at my house. He left before my parents were due.

After lighting the Sabbath candles and eating our roast chicken dinner, Mom asked, "How was Student Day?"

"Ten girls got this National Honor Society certificate and blue-and-gold felt letter."

Dad read out loud, "A faculty committee chooses members based on scholarship, character, leadership, and service." He added, "Congratulations, Dolly!"

Mom asked, "Where will you sew the letter?"

Feeling the soft felt, I answered, "It's cooler to keep it in my drawer."

Mom asked, "Which boys were chosen?"

"Luke, Craig, Jake, Udeh, Neal, Artie, Steve, and five others." Unable to resist teasing Mom by omitting Marcus, I barely kept a straight face.

Predictably, Mom asked, "How about Marcus?"

I playfully looked guileless (an SAT vocabulary word). "Oh, I forgot. He and his cousin are in." Mom gave me a knowing look.

Saturday, May 6, 1961: Milne

After thanking Jed for a lovely red rose corsage, I had a pleasant evening dancing with him at Milne School (run by Albany State Teachers' College). After snacking at Joe's, I enjoyed his goodnight kiss. Recalling Bob's kisses, I marveled that boys I'm not wild about can be fun to kiss.

Monday, May 8, 1961: Shepard

At lunch, I chuckled when Craig said, "Now that Alan Shepard has gone into space, our country won't need me and I can be a lawyer, as planned."

"The height limit leaves me out," Jake remarked with an exaggerated sigh of relief.

"I think I've stopped growing at five-nine, so I'm in. Angela, are you coming with me?" Dominic smiled.

Looking into his hazel eyes, I beamed flirtatiously and nodded, amused that the parents can't prevent my dating a gentile in outer space!

Wednesday, May 10, 1961: Jealousies

At Mr. V's, I praised Sara's help, especially during dreaded family meetings, in obtaining fairer treatment from my parents. I added, "Though obedient Mom was Grandma C's favorite daughter, Mom must have felt hurt and jealous when Grandpa openly favored Sara. Unlike Mom, Sara got out of working in their store and studied music at expensive Julliard. Grandpa kept Mom from studying nursing. People saying that I'm like Sara bother Mom. It's unfair that Mom's insecurities and jealousy about Dad's love for me have made me a scapegoat."

"You understand reasons for your mother's behavior but expect fair treatment?" After I nodded, Mr. V asked, "How about your father?"

"For the year Sara lived with us, she got attention and laughs Dad formerly got from Mom and me. Dad seemed threatened about Sara's influence on me during our daily talks. His jealousy may have prompted his cruel disbelief about Sara's attack. Before my teens, Dad and I were closer. He may be jealous of my boyfriends, but acts warmer than Mom."

"You know reasons for your father's feelings and appreciate his acting more positively towards you?" Nodding, I felt grateful that Mr. V, like Sara, listens respectfully and seems to treat me as an adult.

Thursday, May 11, 1961: Spring Fever

I was glad that Eva phoned. "Angela, this summer I must earn money for the family coffers. We're fortunate to have Dad's disability checks from his job at the post office because my mother brings home little as a hotel maid."

"Eva, I understand. I don't know what we would have done if Mom hadn't been working for the state when Dad was let go."

"On to lighter topics like romance..." We chuckled.

"Bob keeps walking me home, staying to talk, and kissing goodbye really well. He phoned to say, 'I'd like you to be my girl.' After thanking him for asking me, I reminded him that I can date only Jewish boys and added, 'Even if we could date, I'm too young to be serious with anyone.'"

"How did that go over?"

"Who knows? Guys seldom say. Has spring fever hit Schuyler?"

"Not that I've noticed." I giggled before she continued. "Our junior class has about 150 kids. Only about thirty boys in all three years take college prep classes. While I'd enjoy discussing books with a boyfriend, Schuyler's emphasis on sports, unit trades, and commercial classes rules that out. So I'm open to dating an attractive general program guy who seems interested in me."

"He has good taste! We must smuggle you into AHS."

"Thank you! How are your four musketeers?"

"Eva, I love that clever nickname for Craig, Dominic, Jake, and Luke!"

"Which is d'Artagnan?" she inquired.

I laughed. "Ask me after I read *The Three Musketeers*. What's d'Artagnan like?"

"He's the most heroic of the four dashing men of action."

"Passionate actor Dominic may be d'Artagnan. After a lull, I've been grateful for a few recent calls from the musketeers. Brainy senior Jerry asked me to his prom!"

"You'll get to dance!"

"I'm also looking forward to the adult city Tulip Ball! Victor's parents gave him tickets!"

Friday, May 12, 1961: Emblems

Eva and I gave up on seeing a movie because *Hoodlum Priest* and *Return of Peyton Place* didn't inspire us to spend our limited money. She described today's Schuyler recognition day. "The athletic awards took up all but the final five minutes. A *Knickerbocker News* reporter interviewed our football star. The newspaper photographer took his picture with Coach Emerick. In contrast to larger, more costly athletic awards, non-athletes got small emblems for extracurricular excellence."

We snickered about the low value placed on artistic and intellectual activities. "Eva, which emblems did you receive?"

"Dramatics and yearbook."

"Congratulations! They're lucky to have you!"

"I appreciate your cheerleading for my team of one, Angela!"

Saturday, May 13, 1961: Tulips

Huge Washington Park is dressed in thousands of red, pink, white, purple, yellow, and orange Holland tulips. In my favorite aqua formal at the Albany Tulip Ball, I listened to Victor say, "For the first time, I watched the women and scouts dressed in old Dutch costumes and wooden clogs clean State Street hill with wet brooms. My mother said that scrubbing streets before celebrations is a Dutch custom."

"Those clogs look uncomfortable. I wonder how long Albany has had a tulip festival."

"My father said that Mayor Corning started it after World War II."

"Really? I thought it began in the seventeenth century when Albany was Dutch!"

"I heard that Albany is the second oldest settlement in our country."

"Was Albany's first name Fort Orange?"

Victor shrugged. "Do you know Albany's official tulip, which Netherlands Queen Wilhelmina chose?" After I shook my head no, Victor added, "My mother grows the Orange Wonder. It's bronzy orange with red on the petals."

"Is orange a Dutch color because of William of Orange?"

With a blank expression, Victor escaped to a new subject. "The Albany flag has orange, white, and blue horizontal stripes. The coat of arms in the center has an Indian, a beaver...and an old-fashioned ship, like Hendrik Hudson's. The motto starts with A."

"It may be Latin!" Needing to enliven things, I smiled, excused myself, and approached a good-looking young man in a group around the handsome mayor. Getting up my courage, I said, "Pardon me, sir. Do you happen to know whether the motto on Albany's flag is *Amor*?"

His playful grin and twinkling green eyes suggested Irish descent. "I doubt that Albany's money-loving Dutch and English leaders picked love as a motto." With a ready laugh, he raised his eyebrows. "The motto might be *Amor* if the French had gotten this far south…the city flag should be here." I followed him around the large Washington Armory, decorated with colorful pennants hanging from the rafters. Having trailed me, Victor brought up the rear. Locating the colorful flag, our guide read, "Assiduity."

I chuckled about how wrong *Amor* was. "Does assiduity mean hard work?"

"Close enough," the mayor's attendant responded with a smile. I giggled when he added, "I apologize that our fair city isn't more romantic."

After I thanked him, Victor led me onto the dance floor. I felt enchanted to waltz near Albany Tulip Queen Patricia Ponticello in white silk and her handsome partner. About my size with brown eyes and lighter hair, the queen has a vivacious smile. This Albany State senior is the perfect daughter for Mom: a future teacher from Gloversville!

Two orchestras let us dance without breaks! Victor and I foxtrotted past a member of the queen's court in yellow. Her tall, lean partner had fiery red hair and mischievous blue eyes. When he winked flirtatiously at me, my face got hot and I wished for a dance with him. It was exhilarating to be at an adult event with Mayor Corning and society bigwigs! At Herbert's, I enjoyed more excellent dancing with Victor.

Sunday, May 14, 1961: Mom's Day

While eating the breakfast in bed I prepared, Mom approved of the card I made with President Kennedy's quote:

> The American mother, as the heart of the American home, by her labor and love instills in our homes and nurtures in our children the spirit of our country. It is a cherished American custom to devote one day each year to acknowledging publicly our great affection, gratitude, and respect for our mothers.

Saturday, May 20, 1961: No Brothers

Without money to buy clothes, Eva and I browsed in downtown stores. "Eva, hasn't it been a month since your party? Has Xavier apologized?"

"Can you believe that his girlfriend is still with him? Though Xavier has yet to apologize to me, he calls occasionally and chats at school as if nothing happened."

"I might understand males better if you, Doreen, and Tara had brothers instead of sisters." We laughed.

Wednesday, May 24, 1961: Interrupted

Mr. V asked, "Have you communicated to your parents how you feel and what you want?"

"For years! Interrupted before finishing, I usually feel unlistened to. Though they let Sara talk, they usually disregarded suggestions, such as being more flexible. Until escaping to college, I'm stuck under their thumbs. Staying out of their way helps me survive and stay calm."

"How's school?"

"Better and better. I'm lucky that teachers and class-mates are nice to me."

"You feel that you're making the best of your life?"

I nodded. "Others are worse off, like Southern Negroes. I feel so bad about what they go through. I'm fortunate that Hitler, who killed all our European relatives, is gone. I have enough to eat, nice clothes, and a lovely room in a decent neighborhood...but I can't wait to be free to enjoy people I choose."

"As we wind up individual sessions, I wonder how you feel about a joint session with your parents."

"With you there, I'll feel safer talking to them."

Monday, May 29, 1961: Memorial Day

Meeting our Gloversville relatives at Caroga Lake for the holiday was a great chance to catch up with my cousins! Ella asked me, "Do you still miss our aunt?"

"You're a mind reader! I've had weird vivid dreams based on family stuff my mother mentioned years ago."

"We're all ears," said Lydia.

"During the summer of 1933, Sara, age sixteen, took the train to Los Angeles where her parents were helping Uncle Izzy, age twenty-six, recover from an illness."

Ella asked, "What happened to him?"

I replied, "Slower than the other four kids, he was the family scapegoat. After saving money from a Fonda road crew summer job, Izzy ran away at age thirteen. Big and strong, he joined the merchant marine to see the world.

"In my first dream, Sara at sixteen described her exciting trip, including touring movie studios, and showed me Hollywood autographs."

Lydia asked, "Whose autographs?"

"I've forgotten. I should have written down the dream... In September 1933, Sara and Mom, age twenty-one, actually took the train to the Chicago Century of Progress world's fair. My second dream was about Sara, twenty-one, and I, sixteen, taking this fun Chicago trip. After seeing *The Romance of a People* about Jewish history going back four thousand years, our eyes almost popped out watching the police arrest Sally Rand for indecent exposure during her burlesque peek-a-boo fan dance."

"Wow! What do the dreams mean?" asked Ella.

I laughed. "I was hoping that you'd tell me! I want to attend college in NYC and reconnect with Sara."

Ella asked, "How did Sara move to Albany?"

Lydia answered, "Wasn't her husband George an unexciting Albany lawyer?"

I answered, "What a good memory! They married in 1940 after a friend introduced them...On the drive here, I encouraged Mom to reminisce about NYC times with Sara. As usual, she changed the subject."

"Parents are annoying!" Lydia sounded sympathetic. I adore my cousins as substitute sisters.

Tuesday, May 30, 1961: Riders

Advanced American history has reached the present chronologically. Classmates awoke from their slumbers when Miss C said, "The *New York Times* has been covering Freedom Riders. Who can summarize recent events?"

Craig raised his hand. "Supreme Court rulings prohibit segregation on public interstate buses. Brave Negroes and whites, including Yale University officials, have traveled together through Southern states. Ku Klux Klan members and other bigoted locals have set off bombs, rioted, and attacked Freedom Riders to keep Negroes out of white restrooms, waiting rooms, bus seats, and bus terminal restaurants."

After smiling and nodding agreement, Miss C inquired, "How has the government responded?"

Dominic sounded outraged. "Instead of protecting Freedom Riders, state and local police have jailed them for violating local segregation laws, trespassing, and unlawful assembly. President Kennedy and Attorney General Robert Kennedy eventually sent Federal marshals and national guard troops to Alabama to restore order." Tears came to my eyes as I pictured vicious, hate-filled Klansmen beating defenseless riders.

"What leader inspired the riders to protest non-violently?" asked Miss C.

Hank replied, "Gandhi led Indian protests for years until Britain granted independence in 1947."

"Excellent! What will happen next?" queried Miss C.

Marcus said, "I hope that more Federal protection will give riders the courage to continue."

"How long will it take Southern states to integrate transportation, housing, voting, and schools?" asked our teacher.

Jake sounded regretful. "Around ten years, I'm afraid."

"Thanks, Jake. Other opinions?"

I grinned hearing cynical Hank's nasal voice. "Twenty years seems likely."

Did the only Negro girl feel eyes on her? "Maybe I'm too optimistic, but segregation should end by 1966."

Miss C said, "Thank you, Henrietta. Let's vote." Five of us idealists chose five years. Fifteen students picked ten years. Ten pessimists voted for twenty years.

Our teacher asked, "How can citizens hasten greater freedom and justice for all Americans?"

Luke sounded enthusiastic. "Write letters to newspaper editors. Donate and ask relatives and friends to support CORE (Congress on Racial Equality) and the Student Non-Violent Coordinating Committee (SNCC). At age twenty-one, vote for anti-segregation candidates. In college, join freedom rides, if we have the nerve." Because most of us are too chicken, we laughed nervously.

Miss C said, "Good, Luke! How will Freedom Riders affect other countries?"

Udeh responded, "Where discrimination is worse, like South Africa, people might dare to protest non-violently." Doubting that Miss C would support my dating Negro Lee, I smiled wryly while leaving class.

Wednesday, May 31, 1961: Banquet

On the phone, I was glad that Eva reported, "I've dated the Schuyler guy I mentioned. Though he doesn't read books, he's talented at goodnight kissing. What's new? I last heard about the Tulip Ball."

"Bob walks me home and calls sometimes. When he took me to the dramatics banquet, dancing with him and others was fun."

"Did your parents object?"

I chuckled. "I truthfully mentioned getting a ride to a school event. Dad likely appreciated a break from chauffeuring. When Bob brought me home, my parents' lights were off behind their closed door. In the living room, Bob and I danced to low-volume Johnny Mathis songs."

"Did you feel romantic?"

"I need a smarter, funnier boyfriend, but the triumvirate rarely call. Bob aggressively pursues me, but I want to kiss only a boy I love. Though I try to avoid smooching with Bob, he has a way of persisting respectfully."

"I know what you mean. Tired of being virtuous at home, I'm susceptible to a decent boy who offers excitement. With all your time on schoolwork and chores, haven't you earned some pleasure?"

I giggled. "Is that why Bob's kisses are hard to resist?"

Saturday, June 3, 1961: 1936

I sent this to Lydia and Ella:

I can use your opinions about another dream. In 1936, Sara actually attended Julliard and shared NYC apartments with Mom and others on 90th Street and 103rd Street near Broadway. Across from Macy's on 34th Street in a ten-story building, Mom in fact worked for ten dollars a week for Marx Buying Service, purchasing all types of apparel from wholesalers for stores all over the US.

In my 1936 dream, everything seemed like the present, rather than twenty-five years ago. Sara and I, both nineteen, shared an apartment with Mom, twenty-four. Arriving at the apartment in the evening, I screamed after turning on the lights and seeing scores of giant, repulsive cockroaches scurrying for cover. I woke myself to escape. Maybe Mom had yet to discover 20 Mule Team borax powder to get rid of roaches! What does this dream mean? Love, Angela

1936: Coney Island life guard with sisters Sara, 19, & Mom, 24

Monday, June 5, 1961: No

When Mr. V asked our family how things were going, Mom answered, "Things would be better if Angela acted as nice at home as she must at school."

When Mr. V asked me what changes will help our family get along better, I said, "I need freedom to date boys I'm comfortable with. I'll always remember my parents penalizing my good grades and helpful housework by making me miss two Jack Frost dances, one Blue Moon, and two junior proms!"

Mr. V commented, "Mrs. Weiss, you've expressed your desire to feel treated with dignity and respect. The best way you can increase Miss Weiss' respect for you is to allow this change."

Mom looked and sounded spiteful. "Angela can date only Jews."

"Mr. Weiss, for happier relationships, will you approve Angela's request?" Henpecked Dad went along with Mom.

When Mr. V asked what specific changes they planned to implement to improve the home atmosphere, they played the broken record about my socializing with friends rather than with them.

Mr. V responded, "Mrs. Weiss, how can your own behavior be modified to make your company more appealing to your daughter?"

Mom replied, "I'm working as hard as I can at my job and at home. Angela has it much easier. I had to spend my free time working in my father's store. The least she can do is show appreciation for all we have done for her by going out with us."

When Mr. V asked for my reaction, I answered, "The least you can do is show appreciation for an honor student who does over half the housework by letting her date boys she prefers. Because your teen years were unhappy, you're jealously trying to ruin mine."

Mom looked embarrassed to have her motives revealed.

Mr. V asked, "Mr. Weiss, how can your behavior be altered to make Angela more comfortable with you?"

"We've been too nice to Angela. An intelligent girl like her should recognize the importance of dating Jewish boys. People often marry high school sweethearts."

When Mr. V looked at me, I replied, "I've been too nice to clean the house Saturdays, cook and wash dishes nightly, do all my schoolwork, and come here for months while being punished socially. Intelligent parents like you should believe that I want a serious relationship only after college. Without dating freedom, I'd like this session to be my last."

Dad piped up, "We expect you to continue as long as we do."

Mom's tone was punitive. "You need counseling until you learn how to treat your parents better."

Mr. V surprised me. "A sixteen-year-old is almost an adult and capable of making her own decision. Miss Weiss, I'm open to seeing you again only if you come voluntarily."

"Thank you for your time and help, Mr. V! I'd like a break." Faced with my parents' resentful looks, I really appreciated his support, as I did Sara's at family meetings.

Tuesday, June 6, 1961: Upset

The session with Mr. V left me upset and unable to sleep like a log, as usual. Will the parents ever realize that punishing and criticizing me drives me away?

Friday, June 9, 1961: Veep

It's okay that Craig, Luke, and Jake rarely call anymore. I've had to compose, practice, and give an election speech! When Doreen called with congratulations, I responded. "Thank you! I'm in shock! Disliking politics and expecting to lose, I went along with the nomination for speaking practice. Being veep may kill my barely alive romantic life. Though my *dance wheel* got me to the Milne dance and Tulip Ball, I have yet to receive a prom invite. I hope you do better!"

"Thank you! Senior class veep should threaten boys less than eighth-grade school president."

"I'm overjoyed about Craig winning president and Henrietta getting secretary! I'm glad to attend a democratic school which elects Negro class officers."

"Angela, I'm discouraged when Southern whites act so hateful." I agreed before rushing off to usher at senior class night. At the Boulevard afterwards, a gang of us playful classmates had a ball before finals preparation.

Sunday, June 18, 1961: Nureyev

On a study break, I was surprised when Dad excitedly reported, "During the Kirov Russian Ballet Company's Paris performances, star dancer Nureyev defected with help from French officials! The KGB tried but couldn't stop him."

Dad's anti-communist zeal seemed to inspire aqua-feathered Tumba to ham it up. Launching into a lively monologue including I Love You, Tumba nodded his black-and-white head to our applause. After flying to my shoulder, Tumba perched on my finger. I smiled at handsome Nureyev's newspaper photo and hoped to see him dance someday. I'm thankful to live in a free country.

Tumba's profile

Monday, June 19, 1961: Birthday Card

Sara's birthday is coming. I made a card to mail tomorrow.

Thursday, June 22, 1961: Publications

With exams done, I called Eva who said, "Our tests were pretty easy...is Bob still tempting you?"

I tittered. "It's good that I wasn't attached to him. When I got elected class veep, he abruptly disappeared."

"Your popularity must have scared him off."

"So much for male bravery..." We snickered. "What's new at Schuyler?"

"Now that I'm dating, I need Xavier's company less, but his irreverent sense of humor is hard to resist."

"I'm glad that Paul wasn't in on their snubbing and that other boys appreciate you."

"I'm working my way through the fifteen percent of boys in our class named John."

I giggled. "How many have you gone out with?"

"Two out of twenty-three."

I guffawed. "We have a whole year until graduation."

"What's happening at AHS?"

"At tonight's publications banquet, Luke, who has called more lately, was named yearbook editor with Jake as sales manager! At the Moon afterwards, they ganged up on me until I agreed to be assistant yearbook editor."

"Congrats! It's an opportunity to be creative! I've been asked to be Schuy-Log yearbook editor with Paul as art editor. Your Hackett flame Sal will be business manager."

"Congratulations! You'll do a great job! Is Paul still enticing?"

"Definitely, but our class president seems to prefer Catholic school girls. We Schuyler girls must eat our hearts out. Busy on the school newspaper and as Key Club treasurer, Paul plays baseball before working after school."

"Paul is more fascinating than AHS boys. Though Luke has less charm, I'm comfortable with him and looking forward to yearbook time together."

Friday, June 23, 1961: Autographs

Our fun custom of autographing each other's final report cards and envelopes resulted in an *F* in lunch. I was "debarred" from the exam! A *D* in sand piling with 22 on the final made me laugh out loud!

Henrietta, Julia, and I are silly enough to greet each other in homeroom with moos. I laughed at Henrietta's "Good luck to a first-class cow!"

I treasure Jake's note: "Dearest Angela, to the very best: life has to go a long way to give you everything you deserve."

Irene, my beautiful friend since fifth grade, signed: "Best of luck to one of our officers! My vote wasn't wasted. God bless you!"

"May the best the world has to offer be yours, for nothing less is good enough for you!" was Dominic's touching message. Fewer comments about my grades left me feeling happier than last year.

Henrietta

Saturday, June 24, 1961: Prom

Has my *dance wheel* helped me attend four dances this year? Though I hardly know intelligent Forum co-president Jerry, he was a gentlemanly escort to his senior prom. Last evening, I said, "Thank you for the gorgeous orchid! It's my first and I love it!"

Turning a little red, he said, "You're welcome." Like most of the boys, he wore a white dinner jacket and dark trousers. He's about my height with dark blond hair. Though Jerry lumbered around as a dancer, I enjoyed mingling and chatting with the many kids I knew, especially seniors whom I'll miss next year.

Doubling with Doreen and Ty kept the conversation from dying and helped me squelch feelings of going through the motions. Refreshments at Emmy's Brauhaus preceded a long drive to Crooked Lake.

Today, we two couples picnicked and swam at beautiful Lake George. At Doreen's house, doubles ping-pong was fun before miniature golf with laughs! Appreciating attending the prom, I tried to be a good date.

Sunday, June 25, 1961: Calls

I was pleased that Luke phoned. "I have the family station wagon. Let's go for a drive."

Afterwards when Jake called, hockey popped into my head. "How did RPI's hockey team finish?"

"They got to the Frozen Four final tournament where Denver won on its home ice. Though RPI lost to strong Minnesota and St. Lawrence, it was a big honor for a small college to come in fourth nationally!"

"Enthusiastic fans like you must have inspired them!"

Monday, June 26, 1961: Marks

I'm jubilant about final exam marks: English and Spanish II 95, American history 98, Latin III 99, and trigonometry 100 (better than intermediate algebra in January)! A math certificate for honor marks all year, a Latin III reading certificate and certificate for *As* all year, and a Spanish II certificate for *As* all year rewarded my hard work.

At the faculty party, teachers signed our new yearbooks, which include 100 teachers and around 1400 pupils. We kids had a blast dancing and asking classmates, especially graduating seniors, to sign.

At bedtime, I felt warm and happy reading Jake's words: "Dear Angela, Stay as nice and sweet and modest as you are and you'll never have any problems. Love, Jake"

My jaw dropped in amazement at Marcus' comment: "I'll always love you, Angie." He must mean platonically because we haven't talked since the February dance.

This unromantic comment disappointed me: "Best of luck in the future. Keep getting *As*. Yeats"

If I had a crush on Jerry, these platonic words would disappoint me: "Best of luck in the senior year to a girl who doesn't need it. I hope you get the highest average but don't worry about it."

This comment is appealing from a boy I've dated: "I can only say it was fun and I really enjoyed it. Stay as sweet as you are. Love, Victor"

Bob's "Good luck and love always" was good. Did he disappear because he found another girl? I wouldn't be surprised if he was romancing other girls while kissing me.

Tuesday, June 27, 1961: Lee

Last night after admiring Lee's bare-chested wrestling year-book photo, I had this romantic dream which I'd like to come true:

At the Thacher Park swimming pool, my mouth dropped open when I saw Lee's perfect body diving. He must have sensed my stare because he approached me with an irresistible smile. "Angela, I'm happy to see you here."

"Lee, you dive so well!" I felt as if a stupid grin was on my face.

"Thank you! What're you doing this summer?"

"I'm working on Central Avenue in the Classic Shop. How about you?"

"Saving for college, I'm lucky to work construc-tion which pays well."

Ogling his cocoa skin, I smiled flirtatiously. "Your muscles will get even bigger!"

Giving me a slow smile, he looked down into my eyes. "I'll be able to lift you with one arm."

I giggled. "That sounds like fun."

"Do you ever go to Mike's Log Cabin?" he asked.

"If I'm with someone with a draft card. I love it there!"

"I can get in with my cousin's card. If we meet at the Boulevard, we can go to Mike's and dance to the great jukebox tunes." After I nodded yes, he asked, "How about this Saturday at 8 PM?"

"Perfect!" Gawking at his taut muscles, I felt spellbound.

Saturday at 7, I told my parents, "I'm meeting classmates at the Boulevard," before walking there.

Sadly, the dream ended. To dream about the date with Lee, I need to make a *dream wheel* with Lee's name in every wedge! I'd love to actually dance with him, but Mike's admits only white kids. It's so unfair!

Wednesday, June 28, 1961: Prizes

I felt honored to be invited to graduation to receive the Gittel Sanders Memorial History prize, three Latin prizes (Oscar Robinson, Class of 1913, and William Goewey), and a Baird Latin contest honorable mention. The AHS orchestra played *Pomp and Circumstance* as hundreds of seniors marched down the Palace Theatre aisle.

Luke's graduating brother drove me back to their house where Luke, Jake, and I worked on our *Garnet and Gray* yearbook, an enormous project which needs a head start this summer before homework and tests occupy us. After analyzing this year's book and discussing desired changes, Luke took us for a ride. Jake said, "I hope that our football team repeats as Class A title holder. It will be glorious if we top this year's record with more than four shut-outs, a win over archrival CBA, and no losses."

"That would make senior year perfect," I agreed.

"*Per aspera ad astra*," Jake responded.

Luke said, "*Through challenges to the stars.* I like it for the yearbook!"

Being with these intelligent, dynamic boys was more fun than work!

Before I forget I'm recording my junior-year activities: Theta Alpha Literary Society, Forum secretary two terms, Latin Club vice president, *Patroon* newspaper homeroom representative, and homeroom elected representative. Can senior year top this marvelous year?

Thursday, June 29, 1961: Warner's Lake

Without school demands, I'm enjoying my usual summer euphoria. I had fun with Jed, swimming, playing pool, dancing, and eating roasted steak at a lake party!

Friday, June 30, 1961: Rossano

Getting government work papers, I ran into Marcus' cousin and playfully mentioned his resemblance, including curly hair, to Rossano Brazzi, the dashing *South Pacific* movie star.

Sunday, July 2, 1961: Yearbooking

After Dominic called, Luke took me for a cooling mountain drive near Thacher Park. The high was a humid ninety-three degrees! After we worked on the yearbook at his house and picked up his parents, Luke drove me home. I couldn't be happier than to be with Luke, whose creative yearbook ideas I admire.

Monday, July 3, 1961: Honors

Eva and I compared graduation ceremonies, which we attended to receive awards. After congratulating her on an English honor, I asked, "Did anyone else I know win anything?"

"Can you believe that seventy-six percent was the highest French III exam in the class of four? Ric couldn't pick up the prize because he was at Cornell for Boys' State after getting the most votes."

"Schuyler's more democratic than AHS, where teachers picked Marie for Girls' State. Ric must be popular to beat Paul."

Eva chuckled. "Paul beat Key Club president Ric for senior class president!"

"Paul will succeed at whatever he does in life."

"His goal is engineering or something with math."

Tuesday, July 4, 1961: Holiday

I had a great day with my Gloversville cousins at Sacandaga. A swim and long walk let us escape from parents. Lydia shared, "School, including first-year French, stayed easy. I breezed through our advanced classes with good grades."

"How has summer been?"

The corners of her mouth turned up in a mischievous smile. "Some seniors are old enough to drive at night. After working in our store all day, evening parties here on the beach have been exciting, though I can do without the cheap beer."

"AHS boys like beer, too. Ugh! You're lucky to be near a beach! How's that tall, smart football player?"

"I was with Tom at the last party. It was romantic looking up at him and kissing under the stars...we all smoke, too," added Lydia.

"Sara smoked like a chimney. Avoiding smoking is the only advice from Mom I follow. Grandma warned that it's bad for health. It's easy to stay a goody-goody when the cool crowd's unchaperoned parties are forbidden." We chuckled before I asked, "Does your school have nice Negro boys?"

"It's funny that you ask because I'm attracted to the one tall, athletic, smart, popular Negro guy in my classes."

"My romantic dream about a similar guy in my classes ended before our date at Mike's Log Cabin. Even though Mike's is in a Negro neighborhood, Negroes can't enter. When I daydream about slow dancing with Lee, I feel annoyed that the dream can't come true."

"He sounds sexy like my classmate. I wish people would get over being prejudiced."

"When I go away to college, I'll date any boy I want." Lydia nodded in agreement.

Wednesday, July 5, 1961: Dream

Talking about Lee may have triggered this dream:

Wearing a cool summer dress, I entered the Boulevard where Lee said, "With your tan, you look very pretty in white, Angela!" I was thrilled to receive and thank him for a bouquet of purple irises! No classmates blinked an eye when Lee and I left to take a cab to Mike's. After he showed the draft card of his cousin whom he resembles, we went inside and sat in a high wooden booth between dark log walls and the dimly lit dance floor. While Lee drank beer, I enjoyed a red Singapore sling. When the jukebox played Sam Cooke's *You Send Me*, every young couple, including Lee and me, danced. Being in his strong arms was heavenly. While he softly sang the words, I closed my eyes to enjoy the thrill of his hard body glued to mine. Tommy Edwards' *All in the Game* inspired Lee to act out the lyrics by caressing my fingertips and kissing my lips. One romantic old hit after another kept us dancing: *Come Softly to Me* by the Fleetwoods; the Platters' *The Great Pretender* and *My Prayer*; the Five Satins' *In the Still of the Night*; *The Twelfth of Never, Come to Me, When I Am with You,* and *All the Time* by Johnny Mathis; *I Only Have Eyes for You* by the Flamingos; and *our* song, Tommy Edwards' *Secret Love*. With a blissful smile on my face, I was breathless with excitement. My heart was racing when the alarm clock ended my best dream ever.

Anonymous NYC might be the only place where Lee and I could have a real-life date.

Thursday, July 6, 1961: Master

After enjoying a call from Craig, I wrote this:

Dear Cousin Hal,
Congratulations on getting your M.A. degree at Columbia! Your mother wrote that your paper was about Battle of the Bulge German radio propaganda. Wow! You even spent a week in Washington at the National Archives reading translations! While the Germans were broadcasting, Mom was giving birth to me – ha ha! Good luck on your Ph.D. studies! Thanks to your help, I hope to be at Barnard in 1962!
Love, Angela

Friday, July 7, 1961: Raisin

Jed took me to the Delaware for *A Raisin in the Sun,* a touching movie about a Negro family trying to overcome money problems and to better themselves. I love the actor Sidney Poitier whose irresistible smile is like Lee's. Afterwards, the Marcels' *Blue Moon* played on the radio. Jed's brother, who drove, sang well with the hit record. "Blue Moon, now I'm no longer alone, without a dream in my heart, without a love of my own," keeps going through my mind.

Sunday, July 16, 1961: Mike's

Last night and today, I went out with Luke whose grown-up appearance and fake draft card got us into Mike's Log Cabin! Slow dancing to the jukebox made my dreams come true! He clinked his Miller's High Life beer against my delish Singapore sling. "To the yearbook!"

At sixteen, Luke can't drive at night. On the drive home, his brother was enthusiastic about Freedom Riders continuing to fight segregation in Little Rock, Arkansas bus terminals!

Sunday, July 23, 1961: Pittsfield

My family drove to Pittsfield to swim. I felt flattered when boys tried to pick me up three times. Without signs of parental appreciation of my company, I longed to escape when Dad threw a tantrum, roaring at Mom, "For crying out loud, I told you I'd do it! Stop nagging!"

Friday, July 28, 1961: Store

Helping a customer find a dress, I did a double take seeing Craig standing nearby! "How's your job?" he whispered.

Elated about his surprise visit, I murmured, "My nice boss and coworkers, the air-conditioned shop, and all the lovely clothes top last summer's store move."

"Great! Aren't the Jackson, Mississippi Freedom Riders impressive?"

After smiling and nodding agreement, I joked, "Mr. Astaire, I'll be seeing your comic movie tonight. Did you enjoy making *The Pleasure of His Company* with Tab Hunter and Debbie Reynolds?"

I giggled at his reply. "It would have been more fun with you, Ginger!"

After the enjoyable movie, Jed and I snacked at the Waldorf Cafeteria.

Sunday, July 30, 1961: Thacher

With the parents at Thacher Park, I was excited to run into Dominic and family! Swimming with him in the giant pool and admiring his manly athletic body were delightful. He's thrilled about the courageous Freedom Riders!

I felt happy when Luke called later!

Tuesday, August 1, 1961: Fun Labor

I had a ball at Luke's house working on the yearbook with him and a pal before Luke drove me downtown to shop and then home. Though my period arrived, I'm relieved that my cramps aren't bad.

Saturday, August 5, 1961: John

Still happy dating one boy named John, Eva sounded upbeat on the phone. "Since he has a good personality, is fun, and looks good, I do without intellectual discussion, as you have with Victor, Bob, and Jed."

"Eva, you deserve a fun summer!"

Sunday, August 6, 1961: *Exodus*

What a marvelous day working on the yearbook before and after a ride to Thacher, including rum raisin ice cream at Toll Gate! At the fabulous movie *Exodus* with dreamy Paul Newman, lovely Eva Marie Saint, and cute Sal Mineo, Luke put his arm around me when my tears flowed during sad scenes. A taxi took us to the Moon for pizza and home where I enjoyed Luke's goodnight kiss!

Humming the stirring *Exodus* theme song, I was interested in Dad's comment: "*Exodus* is important because it helped end the McCarthy era of blacklisting writers like Dalton Trumbo, who worked on the screenplay adapting Uris's book."

I felt wistful on the two-year anniversary of Sara's attack. Will I ever see her again? She made home happier.

Monday, August 7, 1961: Reading

I said, "Eva, I thought that reading lessons ended with elementary school."

She answered, "Because President Kennedy reads six newspapers daily at twenty-five-hundred words a minute, I'm guessing you're part of the speed-reading frenzy."

"Eva, you're astute! At one-tenth Kennedy's speed, I'm one of the world's slowest readers. You're probably fast without extra training."

"I haven't been timed. If only my feet moved fast, I might be less of a klutz." After I giggled, she asked, "Is speed reading fun?"

"For me, it's hard work. But after class we all kid around with middle-aged, pot-bellied, balding Mr. B and Mr. R, our irreverent instructors from Hackett...On another subject, a new boy from Albany Academy for Boys drove me home and talked for two hours in the car."

"Are you interested?"

"He's nice but I hardly know him. Luke has more of my romantic attention."

"Who knew that working on the yearbook could lead to romance?" We chuckled.

"It seems too good to be true."

"Is Luke typically male in staying mum about the change?"

"You're right! I'm afraid to scare him off by saying anything."

Friday, August 11, 1961: Movie

Jed took me to *By Love Possessed,* a good movie starring Lana Turner and George Hamilton. Glad that Jed has stopped trying to neck or watch TV, I enjoyed his goodnight kiss.

Sunday, August 13, 1961: Fun Sunday

After Luke took me for a ride, I enjoyed dinner with his family before fun work on the yearbook. Our mock-up book is full of ideas for each section!

Tuesday, August 15, 1961: Killing

We teens have confided in teachers Mr. R and Mr. B, who have heard about my crush on Luke, intention of staying a virgin until marriage, and frustration about parental dating rules. After the first class, Mr. B, the married, light-skinned Negro ladies' man who tried to date Sara at the 1958 Parents' Night, said, "I remember your special aunt and recognize you from Hackett."

Tonight, kids joked in Mr. R's office; in Mr. B's office, I heard about his teen years. "Growing up in the Deep South during segregation, I was challenged to survive, let alone have fun." After I reacted sympathetically, he lowered his deep booming voice to ask, "Can you keep a secret?" After I nodded, he alluded to leaving town in the dead of night after stabbing a racist man to death in self-defense. My eyebrows went up and my mouth dropped open in shock as he finished: "I hid in train baggage cars until reaching Philadelphia. The City of Brotherly Love seemed sufficiently large, anonymous, and far north for safety. A possible warrant for my arrest prevents my returning to the South where a fair trial would be impossible, even twenty-five years later."

When the new boy offered me a ride home, I was relieved to escape. Unable to sleep, I pictured nineteen-year-old Mr. B knifing his attacker. Though feeling compassion, I was uneasy about getting on his bad side. He seemed a little dangerous.

Friday, August 18, 1961: Secret

Last night after class, a bunch of kids joked with Mr. B until I was the last one there. Later, I no longer heard kids bantering with Mr. R in the hallway whose light was off. Suddenly realizing that Mr. R had departed without saying goodbye, I felt a little nervous being alone for the first time with Mr. B. His pursuit of Sara and secret killing crossed my mind. Did his charismatic bass voice lull and hypnotize me? Feeling zero attraction to him, I can't understand why I let him try to make me "feel good." No part of me wanted to do it, especially with a lecher like Mr. B who's almost as old as Dad. His explorations left me cold, like being examined by a doctor. When he asked whether I felt good, I said no while trying to look and stay calm. Fortunately, he stopped. I'm lucky to have avoided pregnancy and disease with only his long-fingered, big hand in my private parts. Ich! I'm writing this on a separate paper to hide in case Mom snoops in my diary. This disgusting experience must stay secret even from Doreen and Eva. I'm embarrassed about going along with something I have yet to do with boys I like. I'm ashamed of being a ninny. Why didn't I say no and leave? This is the stupidest thing I have ever done!

Saturday, August 19, 1961: Luke

Today's high point, which kept my mind off Thursday, was a two-hour phone talk with Luke! Relieved that speed reading is almost done, I'll leave promptly with other kids. I thought I could trust a teacher. A teacher acting this way is very upsetting! His poor wife!

Sunday, August 20, 1961: Others

Still in shock about Thursday, I wondered about other poor girls.

Thursday, August 24, 1961: Yearbook

I finished my summer job! Grateful for free time before school starts, I enjoyed hearing Lon's and Rex's yearbook ideas and kidding around at Luke's house Tuesday and today.

Sunday, August 27, 1961: Visit

Despite a few cramps from my period, I had a good day with Luke, who called twice and came by my house.

Packing my pretty green suitcase, I felt a sense of accomplishment about earning and saving $271, over twice as much as last summer.

Monday, August 28, 1961: Belmar

The Levines drove Mom and me south on the Thruway. Poor Dad couldn't leave his new job as Montgomery Ward department store appliance salesman in Menands. We're thankful he's working, though he made more in 1959 at the Surplus Store.

Trying to influence the thoughts of driver Karl and Mom as we neared NYC, I silently repeated *Sara*, until it was too late to visit her. On the New Jersey shore south of Asbury Park, we checked in at Belmar's largest hotel on Second Avenue.

Tuesday, August 29, 1961: Buena Vista Hotel

The hotel stationery advertises Jewish dietary laws observed, an elevator, rumpus room, and Pan American room, whatever that is. I felt sorry for Dad.

> Dear Dad,
> I'm having a nice time here. The ocean is gorgeous. I went in this morning, but this afternoon it was too rough and windy.
>
> How are you? Have you been eating at home or out? Is the porch painted? I wonder how it looks. How has the weather been? Mom is lonesome and misses you already. It's too bad you couldn't come here.
>
> About 120 guests are here and the meals are good, but Young's Gap (Catskills) was better. The heated pool is nice but not large. It's all right that the hotel doesn't have activities because we have the beach and pool.
> Love, Angela

Saturday, September 2, 1961: Date

After a fun beach vacation, we're home on Labor Day weekend. Skipping yearbook labor on a warm, sunny day in the eighties, Luke and I walked to and from the Moon for chitchat with classmates over pizza. I enjoyed his goodnight kiss!

Monday, September 4, 1961: Labor Day

Why haven't my dates with Jewish Luke made the parents nicer, like today at the gigantic Thacher Park pool, an ideal place to enjoy today's high of ninety-one degrees?

1961 AHS Senior

Love is a serious mental disease.

Plato

Sunday, September 10, 1961: Senior Year!

After third-floor sophomore homerooms and second-floor junior homerooms, we seniors have really arrived with first-floor AHS homerooms – ha ha! Not only has Luke called often, but hearing from Craig and Dominic has been wonderful. Prom date Jerry called.

Monday, September 11, 1961: Letter

I got ninety percent on this English assignment about summer activities:

Dear Miss D,
I hope that your summer vacation has been as pleasant as mine.

I must confess that I was fortunate to obtain a job in a women's apparel shop because my mother knows the owner. My work was varied and interesting as were the people with whom I worked. I did stock work: unpacking, ticketing, and steaming new merchandise. I also waited on customers, most of whom were kind and polite, contrary to the usual notions.

The others who worked in the store were, without exception, good to me and very pleasant. I especially liked two college girls from Albany State. One was married; the other was not. One was quiet; the other was an extravert. They both set a fine example and were good company throughout the summer. I often thought that the nicest person I could be would be a combination of these two girls.

The rest of my time was spent in a useful, enjoyable speed reading course. From a mediocre 250 words per minute, my speed jumped to 700. This course I hope will aid me as a senior and in college.

Although enthusiastic about my summer, I am pleased to return to school and see my friends. Though my new schedule will entail hard work, it should prove to be fun.

Sincerely yours,

Angela Weiss

Miss D wrote, "A profitable and pleasant summer. It included some good books?" I should have mentioned many year-book hours preventing book reading. I worried about falling short of expectations after reading: "I am looking forward to our year together. I have heard so many nice things about you!"

Tuesday, September 12, 1961: Rosh Hashanah

After walking me home from our synagogue services, Luke took me to eat at Joe's. His family is less religious; my parents still keep kosher.

On a lovely warm evening, the agreeable Albany Academy boy from speed reading treated me to Stewart's ice cream.

Thursday, September 14, 1961: RPI

Jake called! "Angela, I'm excited because my dad got tickets to attend the RPI holiday hockey tournament again. RPI's great season made tickets scarcer than usual. We hope this year's seats aren't behind metal support columns of the field house, a converted Rhode Island World War II Navy warehouse with only about 4,000 seats. Have you heard of the hockey line?"

"No."

"Until tournament tickets go on sale in September, fans and placeholders line up at the student union waiting to buy up to eight tickets. Frat guys set up beds in line for twenty-four-hour coverage."

I chuckled. "Did your dad sleep there?"

He laughed. "An Irish buddy got the tickets from another Irish guy and so on back to flunkies whom political boss Dan O'Connell paid to wait in line for over a month. The Albany political machine is good for something." I was speechless with amazement.

Friday, September 15, 1961: Necklace

Jerry visited to give me a necklace he bought in Mexico! After thanking him, I enjoyed his trip photos. He asked, "What's new with you?"

"I was elected literary society veep, my favorite position because I'm lazy." We laughed. "How do you feel about starting college?"

"I'm excited. Next week, I'll be a Cornell freshman." Unable to imagine phlegmatic Jerry animated about anything, I suppressed a giggle.

Saturday, September 16, 1961: Indian Summer

I'm relishing a warmer-than-average month without signs of autumn! I hope that Tara gets my birthday card by Monday. Though I see her less because of different classes, I am still very fond of her and will call her tomorrow.

Tuesday, September 19, 1961: Yom Kippur Eve

I appreciated Lon's driving Hank, Luke, and me home from school. Happy that Luke has called daily for a week, I felt elated that he accompanied me to our synagogue tonight. Standing with everyone else while the cantor chanted Kol Nidre for what seemed like hours, Luke and I smiled at each other several times. A ride with Luke made me forget tired feet!

Saturday, September 23, 1961: Football

On a great summery day, Luke and I watched AHS shut out Vincentian 6-0! Last night, we ate at the Moon. Wednesday, he came to my house. Being with him feels so natural!

Sunday, September 24, 1961: Middle

After Luke took me for a ride, we had dinner at my house. My parents approved because he's Jewish.

With the popular first son at NY University, will Luke get more attention from his dad, who works long hours as a Safeway manager? Preferring brainier, creative, earnest Luke, I understand that insecurity makes him toot his own horn, which bothers some classmates.

Luke's petite mom pays more attention to his sweet younger sister. Seeing a middle child neglected and misunderstood makes my lack of siblings less upsetting.

Saturday, September 30, 1961: Conference Plus

The Schenectady yearbook conference with Luke was fun! Learning what local schools put in yearbooks gave us new ideas. Luke and I love and want to maximize more expensive color pages.

We enjoyed the movie *Paris Blues*. Fabulous Paul Newman and irresistible Sidney Poitier played jazz musicians who became Joanne Woodward's and Diahann Carroll's boyfriends. Over a Moon pizza, Luke said, "I enjoyed Louis Armstrong's music in the movie! To be treated decently, American Negroes must live in Europe. It's sad..."

Slow dancing at Mike's Log Cabin was romantic! Luke's sexy masculine physique, open conversation, gentlemanly manners, and warm goodnight kiss made our date ideal!

Tuesday, October 3, 1961: Dating

After a fun Sunday with Luke at our houses, I appreciated tonight's variety: a brief phone chat with Udeh preceded a long talk with Dominic, whom I still enjoy.

When Doreen called, I confided about Luke. "With the Jack Frost dance coming, a bird on a real date is worth three musketeers on the phone."

She giggled. "I've enjoyed dating Logan, an attractive RPI engineering student."

"Wow! A college man!"

"Albany family friends fixed us up after their Massachu-
setts friends who know his family mentioned him."

"I'm happy that a blind date worked! At a mainly male
college, he's lucky to meet a wonderful girl like you!"

Thursday, October 5, 1961: Test

We're lucky to live in NYS, which rewards the highest scores
on today's tough Regents' college scholarship test with a
few hundred dollars a year to attend a college in our state. I
need this money to escape from Albany.

Sunday, October 8, 1961: Steady

When Eva called, I said, "I'm on cloud nine! Luke asked me
to go steady."

She sounded enthusiastic. "I didn't realize that the yearbook romance had become serious."

"I didn't either." We chuckled.

"You've preferred to play the field."

"Eva, my first choice is guaranteed dates every weekend
and for special events with various appealing boys my parents accept. For over a year, I've missed too much without a
boyfriend and weekend dates. I said yes to Luke. It felt right.
I can't wait to attend dances with an excellent dancer who's
not boring!"

"I'm happy for you! A miracle has occurred. Schuyler
won two football games, defeating McCloskey 13-0 and
Lansingburg 19-7."

"Congrats! Everyone must be in a good mood!"

Eva chuckled. "The players got too cocky and Albany
Academy shut us out yesterday at home."

Monday, October 9, 1961: World Series

Dad smiled. "How about those Yankees?" My parents and I agree on something: cheers for the NY Yankees beating Cincinnati four games to one!

Tuesday, October 17, 1961: Dream

Years ago, Mr. J from our synagogue used to pinch my cheeks painfully. I dreamt:

> Aware that Dad earns a pittance in retail sales, Mr. J kindly offered Dad maintenance work at Mr. J's apartment buildings. Staying on at Montgomery Ward, Dad announced at dinner, "I'll do repair work evenings and weekends." Talkative Mom was silent. Remembering Dad's botched attempts to fix simple things, I struggled to avoid guffaws.

The alarm clock woke me. What did the dream mean?

Wednesday, October 18, 1961: Handy

On a sunny, over-seventy-degree day, Luke and I dropped off Doreen's birthday gift, a pretty pin. Continuing to my house, I said, "Last night, I had the second of related dreams. You know that my dad is unhandy around the house. In the dream, he worked part-time doing repairs at Mr. J's rental buildings. Dad's friend Karl phoned Mom, 'Fern, Herm calls continually for advice. He almost flooded a building by misunderstanding instructions! I beg you! Make Herm resign before Mr. J makes him pay for water or other damage Herm causes.' Luke, analyzing these dreams will be good practice for your career as a psychiatrist."

Luke laughed. "I need to learn more in medical school."

Tittering at the image of Dad as a handyman, I mentioned the short-lived bookcase he installed without finding wall studs.

Luke said, "I'm lucky to learn while watching my dad and brother fix things."

"I'm impressed!" A handy husband is a must! Ten days of going steady have been wonderful!

Thursday, October 19, 1961: *Stella* and *Stanley*

Eva joked, "Call me *Stella*."

I chuckled. "Tell me more."

"In dramatics, I was lucky to be *Stella* for scenes from Tennessee Williams's play *A Streetcar Named Desire*. Pregnant, she's crazy about her virile husband, Marlon Brando's role. An intelligent, witty classmate played her husband. Her impoverished, fragile older sister moves into their tiny New Orleans apartment. I must be suggestible because speaking *Stella*'s lines led to my feeling attracted to my classmate."

"You're a talented actress. Did you receive a standing ovation?"

"How did you know?"

"Woman's intuition!" I giggled.

"Even kids not in dramatics are calling us *Stella* and *Stanley*." We laughed. "We're going out this weekend. Before accepting, I called May, his girlfriend who graduated last year, and was surprised to hear, 'Jay and I are pals now. I love you both and hope you hit it off.'"

"She sounds special. Have a fabulous time!"

Sunday, October 22, 1961: Dates

After fun romantic dates for two weekends, I feel overjoyed and lucky to go steady with masculine Luke! Goodnight kissing is blissful with a smart, fun, interesting boy I love who respects and appreciates me enough to go steady!

Thursday, October 26, 1961: Ignorance

At lunch, Dominic asked four of us, "Wasn't poet Carl Sandburg's White House visit great?"

Craig smiled. "I got a kick out of his criticizing Ike for 'talking like a regular Army-trained man.'"

Julia asked, "What was Sandburg talking about?"

Dominic answered, "Our boorish former president called JFK's Peace Corps a 'juvenile experiment.'"

Jake said, "Ike's an ignoramus! Hats off to Sandburg for praising Kennedy's literary and political style."

Saturday, October 28, 1961: Defeat

Luke and I had fun at the football game, even though Schuyler beat us for the first time in seven years! I didn't mind losing 8-7 to Eva's school. While Luke was in the restroom, Eva said that her date with *Stanley* had been fun.

When handsome Paul approached, Eva said, "Here's our president!"

I said, "Congrats, Paul! You'll get good practice for being US president someday!"

Blushing, Paul chuckled. "I'd rather be an artist. Being art editor of our newspaper and yearbook is fun."

I replied, "I love helping plan yearbook page layouts and contents." Grinning down at me, Paul squeezed my arm warmly before turning to waiting female fans.

After Ric joined us, I said, "Congratulations, Key Club president! What are your projects?"

Ric's handsome face lit up. "All year, we're picking up and distributing canned goods for the American Cancer Society. On Thanksgiving, we'll get food from downtown stores, pack it in boxes, and distribute it to needy families. In the spring, we plan to paint a room at a south end youth center."

I said, "Everything sounds admirable!"

Sunday, November 5, 1961: Busy

Laughing, Eva said, "It takes so little to make me happy. We won our fourth football game out of six last night, shutting out Watervliet on their home field."

"Congratulations! Your guys played very well against us."

"At least Schuyler does something right to compensate for being academically abysmal. If our principal had taught math or history, rather than baseball, our curriculum might be more rigorous." We chuckled.

"I'm glad that you're in a good mood! How's your romantic life?"

"It's nothing serious, but *Stella* continues to see *Stanley* who's good company."

"Eva, do you like being yearbook editor?"

"Last month, we took our formal senior photos and candid shots. Lack of time because of dramatics practice and Christmas chorus program rehearsals resulted in Alice's taking over as *Schuy-Log* editor. Though my new literary editor title is a joke, I enjoy writing and editing copy."

"Did Kappa Zeta Phi sorority sponsor a dance?"

"We Kappa seniors delegated all the work to younger girls. Klutzy *Stella* preferred catching up on sleep to attending the dance."

I laughed. "Senior year is the best! Are you still in Future Teachers of America and science society?"

"Only because they require little time. Science society treasurer is easy: we're broke. As elected homeroom veep and member of the safety council and foreign language club, I have no responsibilities. Paul's list is longer despite his after-school job."

"Don't his grades suffer?"

"Angela, he's in Schuyler, not AHS." Giggling, I inquired about Ric. Eva continued. "Dating Marie and an AHS junior, he's become a ladies' man. Xavier's still with Paul's ex. Paul apparently remains the heartthrob of the best parochial school girls."

Tuesday, November 7, 1961: Victory

Luke and I were jubilant watching our talented football team trounce archrivals CBA 19-0! In the fourth quarter, our star Davis Willingham, a speedy, coordinated Negro giant who plays both offense and defense, intercepted a CBA pass on our 12-yard line and ran 88 yards for our third touchdown! What a thrill!

Saturday, November 11, 1961: Model

During Saturday house cleaning, Mom described AHS parents' night. "Your chemistry teacher seemed like an absent-minded professor. He had trouble remembering you."

I laughed. "I'm quiet in my first AHS science class." I omitted that kids cut up in class, taking advantage of the easygoing personality of my first AHS male teacher.

"Your women teachers are old maids. The typing instructor, who looked like a man, called you a very sweet girl whose speed and accuracy are improving."

I bit my lip to keep from blurting, "Your similar short hair looks just as unfeminine!"

Mom continued. "The English teacher said that you write well. Your homeroom teacher was high on you after teaching you Spanish for two years. When Dad asked how you can do better in solid geometry, the math teacher answered, 'Angela's a model student who does her homework and excels on tests.' Why aren't you a model daughter?"

Irritated, I left the room. The Metropolitan Opera's beautiful singing of Wagner's majestic *Lohengrin* music on the radio distracted and soothed me. I was surprised that *Here Comes the Bride* is from this romantic German opera about a knight rescuing a lady.

The excellent movie *Splendor in the Grass* engrossed Luke and me and made me cry. I felt comforted with my head on Luke's shoulder and his arm around me. Identifying with sweet brunette Natalie Wood, I admired cute Warren Beatty.

Sunday, November 12, 1961: Spark of Youth

Picturing last night's movie, I felt glad that our English class read the Wordsworth ode, *Intimations of Immortality from Recollections of Early Childhood*, especially the touching section with the movie title:

Though nothing can bring back the hour
Of *splendor in the grass*, glory in the flower,
We will grieve not; rather find
Strength in what remains behind.

Poignant feelings arise about only seven precious months remaining of my splendid, glorious senior year with Luke. Do Mom's mean criticisms cover envy arising from the loss Wordsworth described of the divine spark or magic of youth? My parents spend most waking hours working to make ends meet. Though Dad avoids complaints, isn't a man with his brains bored?

Friday, November 17, 1961: Acting

Watching the AHS comedy, *My Three Angels* by the Spewacks, Luke and I laughed at Julia, flirtatious Jim, and Bob, who pursued me last spring. While Luke and Lon chatted, I stepped away to congratulate Jim who replied, "Thank you. When will you come to your senses and give up arrogant Luke for your *Osito* (little bear)?"

I giggled. "I expected your girlfriend to see tonight's triumph."

"She had to sing in a school concert. All alone, I need affection from my *Osa Mamacita*."

Un-tempted by Jim, I rolled my eyes. As Luke approached, I beamed happily.

Tuesday, November 21, 1961: Winter

Hurrying home, I felt sad about drab clouds replacing pretty blue skies and dropping over three inches of snow yesterday! Reasons to attend Barnard: warmer weather with less snow; proximity to Sara; anonymity and freedom to date anyone. Though I love Luke, I'm too young to settle down "forever" with anyone.

Thursday, November 23, 1961: Thankful

Driving to Thanksgiving dinner with our Gloversville relatives, Dad said, "Reading about plans to tear down Albany's downtown slums to build state office buildings, I'm thankful that our house is safe from demolition."

Mom said, "Will the state spare our old Morton Avenue apartment building?"

Dad shrugged. "A survey showed that forty-six percent of residents live downtown because it's affordable. Downtown is the only option for twenty-two percent, mainly Negroes."

I asked, "Where will they go if their homes are destroyed?"

Dad responded, "Our millionaire Republican governor, Nelson Rocky Rockefeller, ignores such mundane needs. Though survey respondents criticized crumbling streets and dilapidated buildings, they valued neighborliness. Forty percent like living near friends, compared to only twenty-two percent of uptown and suburban residents."

Friday, November 24, 1961: Enticing Boys

Yesterday, I asked Ella, sometimes neglected because she's younger, "Are you enjoying seventh grade?"

"Changing classes beats listening to the same teacher drone on all day. I'm getting good grades without much studying."

I said, "I wish I could. I must finish all my homework and study hard for exams. Are you in sports or activities?"

Ella smiled. "I joined our synagogue choir."

Lydia snickered. "To get out of working in our store Friday evenings." We three chortled.

Ella said, "Unfortunately, I still miss the dances, but boys my age are uninteresting."

Lydia said, "Ella likes the cute Negro basketball player I snuck out with."

I smiled. "Cuz, you're brave! If I weren't going steady, I'd like to make my romantic dream about intelligent, handsome Negro classmate Lee come true, especially slow dancing at Mike's Log Cabin."

Lydia responded, "The movie date with my Negro classmate was fun but we had too little in common for another date."

"Did anyone look shocked seeing you?" I asked.

Lydia replied, "Who cares? A few girls whispered, 'I wish I had the nerve to date Negroes. My parents would kill me if they found out.'"

I responded, "Those girls sound as chicken as I. I admire your pluck!"

Saturday, November 25, 1961: The King

Nixing Elvis' *Blue Hawaii* at the Strand, Luke and I enjoyed *The King and I*, a great musical movie rerun, at the swanky Hellman Theatre. I like star Deborah Kerr. Bald Yul Brynner who plays the king is handsome. Luke, whose father is bald, is sensitive about his hair thinning on top. Kids tease him. Though Dad's white hair is thin all over, he's not bald. I keep singing the appealing *King and I* tunes, like *I Whistle a Happy Tune, Hello Young Lovers, Getting to Know You,* and *Shall We Dance?*

Sunday, November 26, 1961: College

On a break from memorizing difficult vocabulary words for the SAT in January, I called Eva, who shared, "Thanksgiving was at the house of my younger older sister. Both sisters are expecting. My lovable nephew, who gets into everything, is amusing!"

"You're lucky to have sisters!"

"I love them but their precedent may put even Albany State, let alone law school, out of reach. Working after high school, my sisters married young. My parents are high-school dropouts. Dad said, 'I've done fine working for the post office. Why waste money on college when you'll probably marry? You can work for the state.'"

"But you'll make an excellent lawyer!"

"Thank you, but Mom said, 'I'm too old for hotel maid work. It's time you contributed to the family income.'"

"That's awful, Eva!"

I'm distressed that the smartest female I've known may not finish college! Don't her parents recognize her unique brilliance? What a waste! As a dedicated lawyer, she can help underprivileged people attain justice. Why is life so unfair for girls? If my older sister had lived, Rowena's college expenses might have used up what Dad saved. Eva without siblings might better fulfill her outstanding potential. Feeling luckier to be an only child, I prayed, "Please, God, let Eva graduate from college. I'll trust your wisdom in the future."

Monday, November 27, 1961: Jennie

Eva shared about Ric. "A group of us seeing *Blue Hawaii* ran into Ric. Ric's arm was protectively around giggly Jennie, a slim blonde who's popular with boys. At school concerts, she sings lovely soprano solos. Ric only had eyes for her. It's new to see him infatuated."

"Is she smitten?"

"Though Jennie has gone for bad boys, handsome popular Ric appeals to most girls. I wonder whether Jennie values an intelligent gentleman with a future."

Saturday, December 2, 1961: Holly Golightly

Uninterested in expensive sports like skiing, Luke and I feel fortunate when good movies like *Breakfast at Tiffany's* play. I'd love to look like Audrey Hepburn and appeal to men as she did in this amusing, touching movie. With many boyfriends and an unconventional, glamorous life, her character Holly considered settling down with one man only because she needed money to send to her poor family. Picturing our Hudson River, I'm singing the movie's lovely song *Moon River*, which expresses my yearning: "...off to see the world, There's such a lot of world to see. We're after the same rainbow's end...Moon River and me."

Tuesday, December 5, 1961: Mild

After looking out of the classroom windows often during a productive afternoon yearbook shift, I appreciated strolling home in warmer-than-average, fifty-degree weather; a little rain was better than snow.

Yearbook staff, left to right: Norwegian exchange student Mista, Lon (seated), Jake, Luke (seated), & Udeh

Thursday, December 7, 1961: SAT

Calling Eva about an opportunity to meet at the Albany Symphony Orchestra concert at Schuyler, I wondered why her mom's voice sounded strained. "Eva's not here."

"This is Angela Weiss." She had already hung up. Is Eva all right?

I stayed home to study for the SAT. Though I did well on these College Entrance Examination Board tests last May, higher scores next month should help me get into Barnard.

Friday, December 8, 1961: School Spirit

Our girl cheerleaders led a pep rally for our good-looking basketball team who won their first game against Vincentian (63-47). Luke said, "Tonight's Amsterdam game requires an hour's Thruway drive each way. Unfortunately for our team, few kids are eighteen with cars or otherwise able to attend."

Saturday, December 9, 1961: Jack Frost

Tonight, I was thrilled to finally attend a Jack Frost semi-formal! Rather than waste money on a fussy pastel dress, I wore my black crepe, knee-length sheath with spaghetti straps! The beauty salon set my hair in a bouffant flip.

Committee members Luke, Doreen, Marcus, Neal, Marie, Betty, and my childhood husband Tad worked hard on the dance, including the gorgeous Silver Stardust decorations!

Marsha, two other girls, and I were lucky to be elected to Queen Betty's court! The boys on the court included Lon, Neal, and Tad.

Our talented football players received awards after a 5-3 season, including second place in our tough Class A league!

Everyone regretted that a final-second jump shot defeated our poor basketball team 60-59 last night.

Typically well-dressed, Luke was a heavenly dance partner. Sitting opposite Doreen and Logan from RPI, Luke said, "We're celebrating! Sales manager Jake has gone over the top by selling more than 900 yearbooks, a record this early!"

I commented, "Logan, Jake's an entertaining guy who wants to attend RPI. A fanatical RPI hockey fan, he'll be at the holiday tournament." Looking around, I couldn't find Jake to make introductions.

I experienced *deja vu* when Logan drove us to the Helderberg Mountains in below-freezing weather. After we had drinks at Emmy's Brauhaus, I was relieved that our fabulous evening ended without getting stuck in the snow, as in my scary nightmare!

With Luke

Sunday, December 10, 1961: Disagreeable Parents

Mom wants to experience high school dances vicariously through me. But her frosty Jack Frost interrogation drove me to escape to my room.

I was stunned when Eva's dad said, "She's not here," and hung up before I could ask, "Is Eva performing in Schuyler's Christmas concert Tuesday?" I hope Eva's all right!

Monday, December 11, 1961: No Answer

No one answered several calls to Eva. With snow forecast, I'll skip the concert unless I'm sure to see her. I prayed that Eva and her family are okay.

Wednesday, December 13, 1961: Philistines

At lunch, Craig asked, "Have you heard about America's new cultural low?" After Luke, Jake, Henrietta, and I looked at each other blankly, Craig said, "Even in sophisticated NYC, the Museum of Modern Art hung a Matisse painting upside down for 47 days before someone corrected the error." Everyone laughed.

Thursday, December 14, 1961: Out

When I called to say, "Happy seventeenth birthday, Eva!" her father gruffly said, "She's not home," and hung up. Uneasy, I hoped my birthday card arrived at 106 Jay Street. Has Eva been ill with the flu, pneumonia, or diabetes problems for the last two-and-a-half weeks? My scariest thought was depression or suicide from hopelessness about her future. If girls could call boys, I'd ask Xavier or Paul.

Friday, December 15, 1961: *Patroon* and NMS

When asked by the school newspaper inquiring photographer, Henrietta expressed her opinion well: "The very fact that young adults are willing to try to learn about people of foreign countries and to get them to understand Americans is commendable. Because the group is so young I cannot say if the Peace Corps will accomplish all its ends."

I answered: "The Peace Corps is a wonderful idea. I greatly admire those who are unselfish and patriotic enough to join the organization, which deserves the loyal support of us all." Will I ever become daring enough to volunteer?

I'm pleased to be *The Patroon's Senior of the Issue*. The article mentioned my National Merit Scholarship (NMS) Program letter of commendation. Eight AHS seniors, including Jake, Udeh, and Julia, are among 25,000 US students who won these letters. With over half a million students taking last spring's test, Marcus, Neal, and Hank were among only 10,000 finalists! My letter said that we 35,000 represented less than two percent of all high school seniors. I felt lucky about my four scores in the 99th percentile with social studies in the 95th and science, 93rd. Raw scores totaled 138 and averaged 28; social studies was 26, science 25, English usage 27, word usage 30, and math 30.

Saturday, December 16, 1961: *Carousel*

Luke asked, "Have you seen the movies *From the Terrace, Imitation of Life,* or *Carousel*? I don't have a preference."

"I'd love to see *Carousel*. I've seen the first two more recently." At the elegant Hellman, *June Is Bustin' Out All Over* was cheery! During *If I Loved You* and *You'll Never*

Walk Alone, handsome baritone Gordon MacRae and sweet soprano Shirley Jones made my tears flow. Luke's arm around me felt good.

Slow dancing at Mike's to jukebox favorites like *Earth Angel, Will You Love Me Tomorrow, Georgia on My Mind,* and *Smoke Gets in Your Eyes* was the perfect way to start Christmas vacation! With my limits respected, I enjoyed relaxed good-night smooching on our couch.

Sunday, December 17, 1961: Julia

Calling Julia, who has also stayed friends with Eva, I mooed like a cow. After she mooed back, we both giggled. "Have a great Christmas with your parents and brother!"

"Thank you! How was Hanukkah?"

"I appreciated a pretty white wool skirt and sweater! Have you talked to Eva lately?"

"Not for a couple of months because of play rehearsals."

"You acted so well!"

"Thank you!"

"Julia, for almost three weeks, I've been unable to reach Eva whose birthday was Thursday. During many calls, her parents said, 'She's not here,' and hung up before I could leave messages. Other times no one answered."

"That's frustrating! Her parents have politely taken my messages. I'll try calling."

"Thank you! I'm afraid of her diabetes."

Later, Julia called. "Her mother hung up before taking a message."

"Maybe Eva's helping a pregnant sister over vacation."

"Someone at Schuyler must know...how about Alice from Hackett?"

"I wish I knew her better."

"Angela, I'll call and let you know. Try not to worry."

"Thank you! I feel better after talking to you." Eva's parents reminded me of Sara, trying to get off the phone: "Sorry! Someone's at the door."

Tuesday, December 19, 1961: Christmas Card

Before attending the AHS orchestra and chorus Christmas concert, I sent Eva a Christmas card:

Dear Eva, I wish you a happy and healthy Christmas with your family! I've tried to reach you or leave messages without success. If you're ill, please feel better very soon! I'd love to know how you're doing and whether I can help. I miss you! Love, Angela

Wednesday, December 20, 1961: Candy Please

Last night's scary dream recreated an actual 1958 classroom emergency I heard about: Eva's blood sugar got dangerously low. Classmates had to find Eva something sweet to eat before she passed out.

In my nightmare, Eva looked very ill. Before I awoke, we kids were scrounging around for candy. Feeling uneasy, I need Sara's advice.

Thursday, December 21, 1961: Fears

In our dark booth at Mike's Log Cabin, I confided in Luke about Eva whom he hardly knew in our ninth-grade home-room. After I thanked him for listening and asked advice, he replied, "Have you gone to her house?"

"Good idea! I'll try to get up my nerve."

"Shall I come with you?"

"Yes! You're the best boyfriend and a great future psy-chiatrist! Thank you!" Putting his arm around me, he kissed me gently before our bodies joined on the dance floor. It was heavenly!

Sunday, December 24, 1961: Magic

After sleeping like a log for about nine hours, I quickly wrote down my extraordinary dream to prevent forgetting:

Though I looked normal (for me), I had magic powers as a descendent of King Arthur's Merlin and of Salem witches. To make things better for Eva, I waved my sparkly silver wand, which resembled the Jack Frost dance decorations. The magic cured her diabetes and changed her parents' minds: they let Eva complete college while living at home without working. I saw a vision of Eva as a lawyer arguing a case at the Supreme Court.

What a letdown to awaken and realize that it wasn't real!

Monday, December 25, 1961: Christmas

On a below-freezing day, Mom roasted the turkey and I prepared the stuffing, green beans, and salad of lettuce and tomatoes. Aunt Myrna brought her delicious green apple pie!

In my room afterwards, Lydia shared news. "My election as sophomore class treasurer has brought attention from cute older boys, including an invite to the fall harvest dance!"

"Congratulations! Was the dance fun?"

"Wonderful! Even wearing heels, I looked up at my date, a part-Italian basketball player who's an excellent dancer. During vacation, rides from seniors with cars have let us sophs enjoy skating and skiing."

"You're lucky to go with seniors. As a sophomore, I was too shy with them to think of anything to say."

Lydia chuckled. "If Gloversville girls party, older boys ask them out."

I laughed. "After rarely dating as a junior, I feel lucky to canoodle with a great boyfriend and avoid pressure to do anything risky."

Wednesday, December 27, 1961: Visit

On an above-freezing day, Luke and I walked fast for almost two miles to Eva's row house. Around one-thirty, we rang the upstairs doorbell and knocked on the basement door. Though the house looked dark and deserted, we kept trying for a half hour. "Luke, maybe she's still away for Christmas at a sister's house."

Thursday, December 28, 1961: Alice Said

Julia called! "Angela, I finally reached Alice whose family was away."

"Thank you for all the time you've spent."

"I had nothing better to do." She chuckled. "Eva was in school until the end of November. Alice said, 'Eva is so talented. The magical lilt in Eva's voice makes whatever she reads aloud in English class more touching.' Alice will let me know whether Eva's back in January."

"Julia, you're sweet to call Alice and me!" After describing my visit to Eva's house, I felt too nervous to end with a silly moo.

Friday, December 29, 1961: Deserted

On this sub-freezing day when Luke had the car, we were discouraged to find no one at Eva's house. Yearbook work helped distract me from worrying.

Saturday, December 30, 1961: Slow Dancing

Luke and I enjoyed running into Craig and other classmates at Mike's Log Cabin. Dancing with Craig again was fabulous. Accustomed to Luke, I was conscious of Craig's usual lack of male reaction when a slow dance brought our bodies together.

Sunday, December 31, 1961: NYE

My 1960 New Year's Eve wish to be dancing tonight with a boy I like romantically miraculously came true! Luke's pal's party included dancing to hits like *Runaround Sue* by Dion, *Big Bad John* by Jimmy Dean, *Please Mr. Postman* by the Marvelettes, and *The Lion Sleeps Tonight,* an odd tune I like by the Tokens. During an extended midnight kiss, I felt euphoric. Dancing to the romantic classic *It's All in the Game* by Tommy Edwards ended a perfect evening.

1962 AHS Senior

When we remember we are all mad, the mysteries disappear and life stands explained.

Mark Twain

Monday, January 1, 1962: Resolution

I'm a crazy, mixed-up kid pulled in different directions. I'm having the best time of my life with an ideal boyfriend, special classmates, and interesting activities. I'll be sad when the exciting social life, lighter class load, and reduced grade pressure of my magnificent senior year end.

In Albany, I'm known and treated well. I appreciate a feeling of belonging when I run into people I know. In the bigger world, will I receive colder treatment?

Controlling parents, frigid winters, conventional attitudes, and the inhibiting lack of privacy motivate me to escape Albany. Everyone knows what everyone does and gossips about it. I'm a caged bird eager to fly away and be free to date anyone I find interesting.

Though I yearn to be on my own, the need to earn money will interfere with freedom and time to do as I please.

The parents exasperate me about dating Jews, but at least they support education for girls. I'm horrified that the parents of the most gifted girl I know consider college a waste for females! I pray for Eva regularly and hope that she's well. My New Year's resolution is to appreciate my parents more and remember that they could be worse. I'm thankful for Dad's seventeen years' savings in my college account and my summer job earnings. Although college requires much more money, scholarships may help. In my poor family, being an only child is best. A sibling, especially male, might consume the limited funds.

Thursday, January 4, 1962: Missing

After I mentioned my second visit to Eva's house, Julia reported:

> Eva hasn't returned to school. No one's answered Alice's calls to Eva. Paul, Ric, and Xavier shrugged when Alice asked for Eva's sisters' married names. When Alice asked where Eva is, the dramatics teacher's gaze shifted as if she knew something she wanted to conceal. Alice admitted she could be wrong because of Miss M's wandering eye.

When I couldn't resist mooing in frustration, Julia smiled and mooed back. "Julia, thank you for this progress! If I were as smart as mystery novel detectives Nancy Drew and Cherry Ames, I'd know how to solve *The Case of the Missing Senior*. Can you think of anything?"

"Let's keep phoning." What would Sara suggest?

Friday, January 5, 1962: Nightmare

I felt shook up after my recurring nightmare:

> I'm chased by a criminal who keeps gaining on me at night in the rain on slum streets, maybe in NYC. Running as fast as I can, I am terrified hearing his footsteps behind me and dread being grabbed. To escape, I wake myself up.

Relief flooded my body though my heart still pounded with fright. Am I afraid of not knowing exam answers this month? It's time to start cramming!

Saturday, January 6, 1962: Twenty-Five

Talking loudly, drinking, and snacking, relatives and parents' friends seemed to enjoy the twenty-fifth anniversary celebration at our house. The crowd hushed when stunning Cousin Beth made a grand entrance into our modest living room. Snowflakes dusted her wavy copper hair. Karl Levine jumped up to help Beth take off her fur coat. He looked enthralled as he gazed into her big brown eyes and eyed her shapely figure. I chuckled when he asked, "What's a glamorous redhead like you doing here? Do you live in Albany?"

"We do." Her smile was charming.

"We?" Karl asked.

"My husband and daughter are here." Adorable June, age six, played on the floor nearby with the bongo drums Sara gave me.

"Lucky man! How about a drink?"

Beth asked, "Rye and ginger?"

Karl grinned. "I can offer a Manishevitz wine highball. The Weisses aren't big drinkers."

Wearing my parents' birthday gift (small gold and garnet heart on a chain), I complimented Beth. "I like the triangular shape of your silver and gold sail boat pin!"

"Thank you, Angela. On Long Island, sailing our boat was delightful." Sad that her young doctor husband died of a heart attack, I nodded.

Mom piped up. "On the first occasion since our wedding that Herm's and my family are together, we're also celebrating my birthday and Angela's seventeenth birthday!"

She ignored Karl's "Are you turning thirty, Fern?" People laughed, clapped, and cheered.

Cousin Hal proudly introduced his pretty, blue-eyed fianceé. "Eileen is an outstanding writer and English major who's been active in Barnard literary circles."

I smiled. "I love your sparkling engagement ring!" Blushing, she thanked me. I was too shy to ask about the wedding date.

Before leaving for Gloversville with their parents, Lydia and Ella quickly dried an unending stream of dishes I washed. My red-plaid apron protected my lovely Hanukkah outfit. The pale fur blend pullover feels like cashmere!

When only Cousin Ron and his parents remained, he said, "After hearing good things about Angela's other cousins for years, I appreciated meeting them, especially Lydia and Ella." I laughed when he commented, "It's good that the guests devoured most of the popcorn, pretzels, nuts, chocolate candy, crackers, cheese, apples, pears, grapes, and anniversary cake. We have less to clean up and put away." Drying the final batches of dishes, Ron made the time pass enjoyably by describing his busy social life.

I said, "I'm happy that your senior year has been sensational! I adore Hal's fianceé!"

"We all love Eileen and are very happy for Hal! She has beauty, exceptional intelligence, a fun sense of humor, and a marvelous personality!"

Regretting Sara's absence, I wondered whether Mom missed her only sister. Tumba's chirping cheered me up.

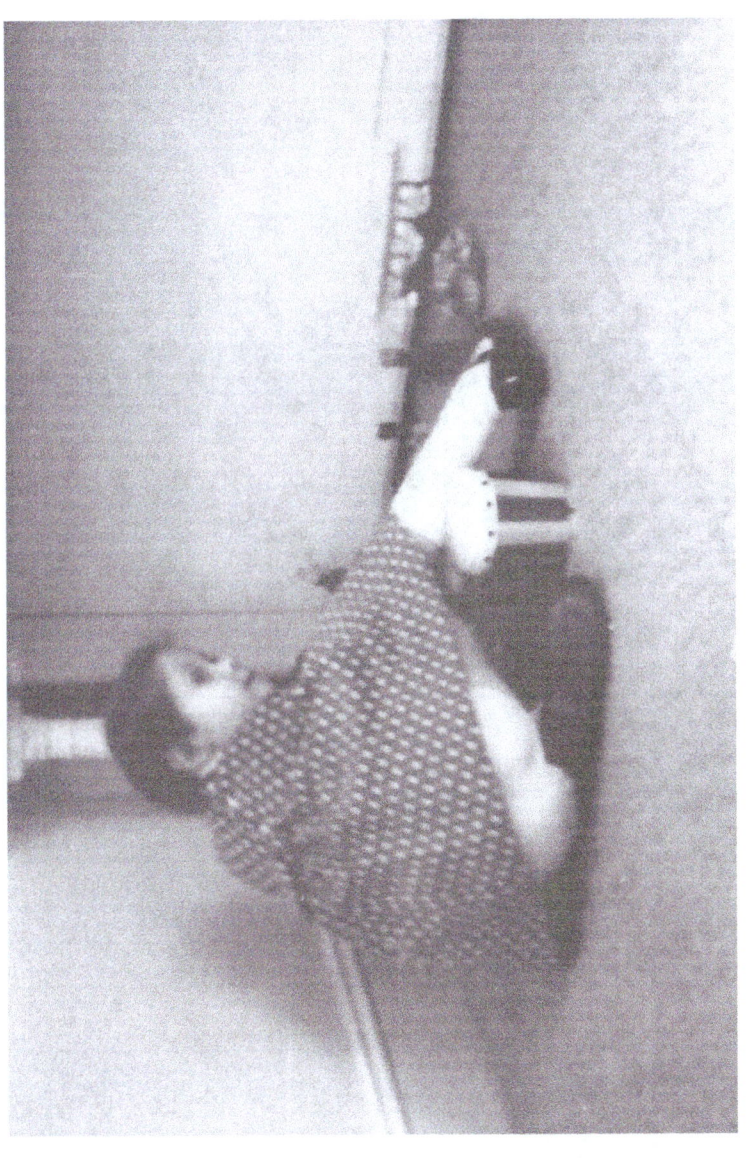

June near our piano

Front row left to right: Beth, June, me; middle row left to right: Ella, Mom, Dad, Eileen; back row left to right: Uncle Abner, Lydia, Beth's husband, Aunt Myrna, Aunt Lila, Uncle Bert, Aunt Rhoda, Hal

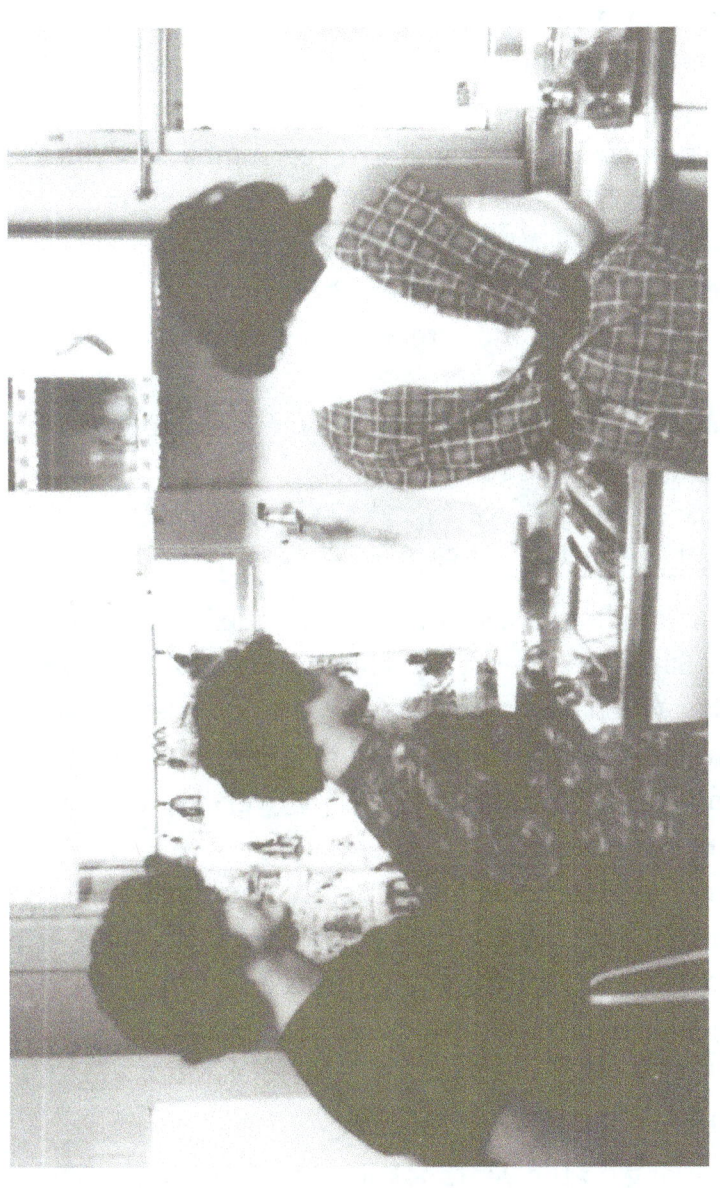

Cousins slaving away

Sunday, January 7, 1962: Birthday

My rainy seventeenth birthday felt like spring with the temperature above forty! Ron's presence made it special! He got along well with Luke who came for birthday cake with my family.

Luke's deep voice saying, "Hello, Tumba!" seemed to inspire our parakeet to ham it up; he clearly uttered Happy Birthday and I Love You more than once.

When Aunt Lila said, "His little voice sounds cute," Tumba puffed out and preened his turquoise feathers. Everyone laughed.

At bedtime, my usual *Shema* prayer in Hebrew and English preceded prayers for Eva and Sara.

Monday, January 8, 1962: Ella

I enjoyed reading Ella's birthday gift, the short story she gave me Saturday. Almost my height, she's a talented writer. Yesterday, when Ron asked me why Ella's circle pin was on her right lapel, I said, "Maybe the meaning in Gloversville is the opposite of Albany and NYC. Only twelve, she has yet to mention a boyfriend."

Chuckling, Ron teased me. "Before you turned thirteen, you married Tad; were in love with Edwin, Ray, and Artie; and had other boyfriends and crushes."

I giggled. "But my pin stayed on the virginal left."

Wednesday, January 10, 1962: Jake

After working on the yearbook, I asked Jake, "How was the RPI tournament?"

"Good, but less exciting than last year when RPI won. Hockey powerhouse Michigan beat RPI, which defeated McGill and Yale. We got hoarse cheering. If RPI accepts me, I'll attend more games next year."

"They'll be fortunate to have someone as smart and conscientious." Luke agreed when I added, "You're a great sales manager!" I'll always be fond of special Jake!

Friday, January 12, 1962: Pudding

For Mom's fiftieth birthday, I baked rice pudding with cinnamon in a square pan. After she blew out millions of candles and we sang *Happy Birthday*, she said, "My last birthday wish came true! I'm finally getting paid more fairly for private secretary and administrative assistant work for two department heads."

I asked, "Wasn't it four?"

"I regret losing psychology, but not farm. I like occupational therapy and education services. With the bosses visiting mental hospitals and state schools most of the time, I love being in charge, including improving report forms. Every other month, I compile and edit the occupational therapy newsletter from material in the monthly reports from thirty-four state institutions."

"Do your bosses change what you write?" I inquired.

Mom laughed. "No. Busy with more important work, the director and assistant director are relieved to avoid doing it. They trust my judgment because the institutions compliment my newsletters."

Sunday, January 14, 1962: Let Down

While Luke had the car, we swung by Eva's house. When no one answered, Luke's hug helped me feel less anxious.

Monday, January 15, 1962: Prep

I've had *B*s in typing and solid geometry and *A*s in English and chemistry, where our teacher lectures and does experiments below our tiered seats while jokers cut up. I'm memorizing the periodic table elements and rereading class notes and important sentences in textbooks. Stuck prepping for exams, I'm okay with high temperatures well below freezing.

Sunday, January 21, 1962: Apprehensive

While studying, I've continued to feel helpless and upset after calling Eva regularly without messages taken when a parent answers.

Saturday, January 27, 1962: *Pinocchio*

To celebrate the end of exams, Luke and I attended a Palace Theatre matinee. A kids' movie was better than boring Westerns. At least it was above freezing as we chatted with Schuyler kids we bumped into. Dazzled by Paul's smile, I was amused that his date from St. Joseph's Academy possessively hung onto his arm.

To Ric, I said, "Congrats on being a celebrity! I saw your newspaper photo."

Blushing, Ric thanked me. Looking smitten, he introduced pretty, petite Jennie.

After we discussed the movie, which first played before we were born, I asked Ric, "Is Eva still out of school?"

He looked away. "As far as I know."

"I'm concerned. Is she all right?"

"I'm the wrong guy to ask. She's in the dramatics and music crowds."

"Aren't you in those clubs?"

He chuckled. "But I party less."

"When I've tried to leave messages, her parents have hung up. Can she be in the hospital?"

Smiling, he shrugged, put his arm around Jennie, and led her away. I had the feeling that Ric knew more.

Key Club president Ric receiving an American flag from Kiwanis Club officials

Monday, January 29, 1962: Impure

In the cafeteria, Jake looked mischievous. "Angela, I'm glad that we danced the twist at Dominic's party a year ago." While trying to figure out his meaning, I felt my brow wrinkle.

Dominic jested. "Jake, have you quit twisting because it's now impure?"

Jake grinned. "I'm thankful to be at AHS and free to do any dance. All I need is a girl who doesn't mind having her toes stepped on."

Everyone laughed before I asked, "What happened?"

Taking pity on ignorant me, Craig explained, "The newspaper reported that the Buffalo NY Catholic bishop has banned twisting from Buffalo Catholic schools. Only pure dances are allowed."

Jake led a round of snickers.

Dominic saw me shake my head. "A penny for your thoughts, Angela."

"I need more than pennies to pay for college." I joked to avoid admitting that slow dancing glued to a boy's body seems more wonderfully impure than the athletic twist without body contact.

We laughed at Craig's quip. "Chubby Checker wrote the bishop a thank-you note for helping boost his twist record sales."

Tuesday, January 30: Grades

I was relieved to get 99 in chemistry, 98 in solid geometry (despite *Bs* on two six-week report cards), and 98 in typing. Will 90 (barely an *A*) in English hurt my Barnard chances?

Tuesday, February 6, 1962: Basketball

The limited amount of snow in January was too good to last. Luke said, "If the weather was better and the game closer, we could cheer on our basketball team to keep Mont Pleasant from replacing us at third in our Class A league. AHS is favored."

I asked, "Is Linton first as usual?"

"Yes, with Amsterdam second."

Thursday, February 8, 1962: Disappeared

Luke skipped our AHS play *Our Town* by Thornton Wilder. During intermission, I smiled at Craig and said, "I'd appreciate your opinion about a recent dream."

"Just call me Freud."

I giggled. "The dream occurred during our twentieth reunion weekend. Friday night, we class officers attended *Cinderella,* a community play. Recognizing the lead actress scrubbing the hearth, I gasped, 'Ee.' You clapped your hand over my mouth to prevent my further disrupting the play by blurting 'Va.' During the Saturday reunion dance, I was stunned to pass Eva, dressed as a maid, near the ladies' room. When I complimented her *Cinderella* acting, she called it a 'busman's holiday,' and added, 'I took over Mom's job cleaning Ten Eyck Hotel rooms when lack of money forced me to quit college.' When I inquired about her health, she replied, 'It's okay.' After I asked whether illness made her miss school during senior year, she mumbled, 'I must catch the last bus,' and limped away."

Looking surprised, Craig said, "I've been too busy with class president stuff to call Eva."

"During the two months she's been absent, I have yet to find her at home or get her parents to leave a message. Alice was in the dark when Julia called. When I ran into Ric, he came across as evasive. What does the dream mean?"

"Eva's limping suggests physical disability. Maybe diabetes is keeping her out of school."

"That makes sense. I wonder whether she'll attend the Schuyler Sno Ball Saturday."

When Craig said, "I'll find out," I felt better and thanked him.

Sunday, February 11, 1962: Mystery

Craig reported, "Paul seemed unclear about why Eva's gone. She missed the big dance. Ric avoided disclosing anything. I got the impression that Xavier knew something. He kept talking about professional basketball and baseball, despite my disinterest in them!"

After chuckling, I said, "You've been kind to call the boys!"

I wrote to Eva: "Craig, Julia, and I miss you a lot. Please let us know how you are. Can we help? If you're ill, get well as soon as possible! Love, Angela"

"Sorry! I'm late," said Eva's mom before hanging up again! Will this mystery ever end? After over two months, I'm more fearful than ever about Eva!

Monday, February 12, 1962: Eighteen Below and Spies

Dear Diary, can you believe that it was eighteen below zero yesterday? This harsh weather has destroyed any sentimental feelings for Albany.

I agreed when Luke commented, "Luckily, we had Russian spy Rudolf Abel to exchange to bring our spy Gary Powers home safely!"

Tuesday, February 13, 1962: Valentines

I'm lucky to have a romantic boyfriend who sent two fancy Valentines signed love and will take me to the movie *Tender Is the Night* Saturday! I loved this F. Scott Fitzgerald novel about a psychiatrist who falls in love with and marries his patient. Sara and Mr. V have influenced me towards a career in psychology. Is this common for people who feel unappreciated at home?

Wednesday, February 14, 1962: Jackie

I was enthralled watching our marvelous First Lady on our neighbors' TV. Describing her historical research, Jackie conducted a superb tour of her authentic White House restoration! To save tax dollars, she charmed antique collectors and experts, decorators, and organizations into donating furnishings and services. I admire her so much!

Thursday, February 15, 1962: Winners

The *Knickerbocker News* carried a long article: *520 District Seniors Awarded Regents Scholarships.* I tittered at Mom's rapture about Marcus ranking tenth in the whole state and first among 256 Albany County pupils winning four-year scholarships. She's probably designing wedding announcements and fantasizing about hugging him as a son-in-law.

I'm eager to congratulate Hank (fourth in Albany County with 261), Craig, Jake, Julia, Cara, Udeh, Lon, Marie, Neal, and Steve. A top student like Luke should have been among the 25 AHS winners. Twenty percent of 16,000 taking the test in NYS succeeded.

Why was the first girl in Albany County (me) listed as sixth? I had the same 259 score as the boy listed fifth. The article, including a photo of and paragraph about each top-six winner, mentioned my NMS commendation letter and interest in Barnard and psychology. Mom is sending copies of the article to relatives.

At Schuyler, only Eva, Ric, and Xavier won. I felt sad that no one answered my call to congratulate Eva.

Saturday, February 17, 1962: Vietnam

On our date, I asked Luke's opinion about *It's a Real War in Vietnam* from the newspaper:

> President Kennedy came closer at his press conference to answering questions about the war in Vietnam. How deeply are we involved? American soldiers in Vietnam have been ordered to fire back if fired upon. The Republican National Committee has suggested (it) could turn into 'another Korea.' To retain American popular support for the Vietnamese effort, the government must 'let the people in on it,' (without) tip(ping) our hand to the enemy and overpublicizing what we hope to keep a limited war.

When Luke replied that he trusted President Kennedy more than anyone to use the best judgment to keep our country safe, I agreed.

Sunday, February 18, 1962: Valuables

While neatening my closet and drawers, I appreciated my silver charm bracelet and other *real* jewelry. The gold and tiny garnet baby ring from Grandma C fits on my pinky. Because her 1930s white gold and onyx pinky ring with a tiny diamond is too small for Mom, I have it! I inherited Grandma W's cuckoo clock pin with tiny pearls, rubies, and an aquamarine. Luke knows that the marquise-shaped aquamarine and white gold ring I love to wear is from Mom's boyfriend before Dad.

Wednesday, February 21, 1962: Ride

Chilly wind made me accept a ride from Jim who lives four blocks away on Woodlawn Avenue. Parking in front of my house, he flirted. "If you get over your crazy infatuation for Luke and go out with me, imagine the fun we can have, including the junior and senior proms!"

I smiled. "How about your girlfriend?"

"We broke up because I can't stop thinking about my *Osa Mamacita*."

I shook my head in disbelief. "Does she know that you've broken up? You've mentioned the special favors she gives you."

"No one can compare to you, *mi queridisima (my dearest)*. Ever since Spanish class last year, you've been my dream girl. Luke takes for granted his good luck in having you. I feel like punching him in the nose when he flirts while you slave away on the yearbook. Presiding over Foreign Student Exchange (FSE) meetings, he personifies *Power Corrupts*, especially with the veep."

I chuckled. "Is the junior class president the pot calling the kettle black?"

He couldn't help laughing. "My sweet Valentine, when you get over Luke, *el caballo con uno cuerno, su osito* (the unicorn, your little bear) will be waiting." Before driving off, he surprised me with a hug and peck on the lips. Though popular and loads of fun with a good imagination and brains, he can't be trusted with girls. Debating and acting talents make him dangerously charming and persuasive.

Thursday, February 22, 1962: Nicest

Is Luke's insecurity about missing an NYS scholarship making him play around? Though he was voted biggest flirt in our Hackett homeroom, I'm not jealous because he's my best-ever boyfriend. Together on most Saturdays and daily in the yearbook room, we're in the same advanced classes. Today, Luke nodded, smiled, and grabbed my hand when his best pal said, "Luke, Angela's the nicest girl you've ever taken out. Angela, I'm privileged to be your friend." Feeling gratified, I beamed and thanked him. Luke seems to sincerely care about me.

Saturday, February 24, 1962: Blue Moon Dance

As Luke and I whirled to the music of Phil Foote's band, I admired the dramatic Blue Mist dance theme background and felt glad that my old friend Irene was queen. I adore big dances with Luke, who's very skilled at turns and dips. Enjoying the white roses wrist corsage he generously gave me, I felt proud of an escort who looked sharp in a dark suit and narrow tie. Below-freezing temperatures made it hard to stay warm in my strapless aqua gown and little white gloves. Eight inches of snow meant changing from high boots into aqua satin heels. Tons of beauty parlor hairspray prevented my bouffant flip from wilting. Here's to summer weather at the senior prom!

Luke & I enjoying his generous white corsage

Wednesday, February 28, 1962: Sweet Tooth

Jake has kept us informed about how many Mason candy boxes have sold since Valentine's Day to help finance yearbook extras like padded hard covers for seniors. The insatiable sweet tooth of AHS buyers of coconut almond, chocolate mint, and assorted jelly is astonishing. Contrary to its apathetic reputation, our senior class has become an enthusiastic sales staff, partly because some proceeds go to FSE. Everyone adores our foreign exchange student: smart, athletic, modest Mista.

Mista from Norway

Thursday, March 1, 1962: Ninety-Ninth Percentile

I'm glad that much colder-than-average February is past and thrilled about SAT scores beyond my wildest dreams, though I can't tell anyone. Surprise: math increased to 715 from last May's 640! I'm grateful to raise verbal aptitude from 686 to 698 and English achievement from 680 to 770! Happy with last May's 742 on social studies and 673 on Latin, I skipped repeating them. Does anyone get perfect 800 scores?

Saturday, March 3, 1962: Supportive

Luke's done so much to make me happy this year that I feel good as his supportive listener. I easily omitted my SATs while enthusing about his improvements. When confident at school, Luke's at his best.

Tuesday, March 6, 1962: Statistics

Luke and I chuckled at today's school paper. Starting with the US population of 175,000,000, the article subtracted retirees, students, government employees, armed forces, prison inmates, mental and other hospital patients, and bums and drunks. With only two people left to work, the author concluded, "You better get busy because I'm tired of running this country alone."

Wednesday, March 7, 1962: Eva

Though discouraged about a huge snowstorm, I was elated when Craig said, "Paul said that Eva's back in school without signs of illness."

"Craig, thank you for the wonderful news!"

Julia and I mooed happily about Eva's return!

Hearing Eva's voice, I breathed a giant sigh of relief! Busy studying for a test, she invited me to a matinee Sunday. I can't wait!

Thursday, March 8, 1962: Score 38-23

Luke and I got stomach aches laughing at the faculty-football team basketball game with hilarious male student cheerleaders attempting high kicks while dressed in tatters. Though expecting our basketball coach, despite a beer belly, to shoot well, we couldn't believe that a music teacher and a shop teacher scored more than most of our football players.

Saturday, March 10, 1962: Flambé

My parents, Luke, and I celebrated Dad's and Luke's birthdays with a yummy dinner at Jack's Restaurant. At 42 State Street, Jack's opened in the Dark Ages when Mom was an infant. I liked the starched white tablecloths and napkins. My Manhattan clam chowder and filet of sole were delicious. Luke enjoyed crab cakes with coleslaw. We shared perfect French fries. Mom, always on a diet without getting thin, ordered chicken breast. Dad's dinner was fun. The polite waiter, dressed in a tuxedo, flambéed the sauce with brandy at our table. When the tall flames died down, he poured the sauce over filet mignon steak slices and mushrooms.

Dad asked, "Did you know that *My Fair Lady* was the hottest show in Albany for twenty minutes recently? The audience of 1,200 was unaware of anything unusual until after the final curtain."

Looking puzzled, Mom inquired, "What does that mean, Herm?"

Dad explained: "Smoke poured into the street from the Palace Theatre cellar. A passerby yelled 'Fire!' Firemen prevented smoke from becoming a fire while Palace staff professionalism prevented a panic."

We chuckled at Luke's jest: "I'd prefer a *cooler* version of the play."

Dad asked, "How's the AHS basketball team doing?"

Luke replied, "We're happy with twelve wins, including one over powerhouse Linton, and six losses."

Dad commented, "Twice as many wins as losses is impressive. Can the Yankees repeat as World Series winners?"

When Luke remarked, "Matching 1961 will be hard," I nodded picturing the cutest stars: Roger Maris and Mickey Mantle! After dessert, I tittered when Dad, who claps at home after tasty meals, put up his palms to approve. Remembering where he was, Dad stopped himself in time.

Sunday, March 11, 1962: Smoke

After Eva and I saw Geraldine Page suffer from unrequited love of handsome Laurence Harvey in Tennessee Williams' *Summer and Smoke*, I felt emotional. After lighting a cigarette, Eva said, "It's just as well that I can't act in our senior play. Page's performance made me feel inadequate as an actress."

"She was outstanding, but so are you! Is your health all right?" I was bursting with curiosity.

"Thank you. I'm making up months of schoolwork to avoid an unbearable extra year at Schuyler."

"Did you receive my cards and note? I missed you!"

"Yes! Thanks, Angela!"

"When your parents answered a few of many calls, they hung up without taking messages. On several visits, no one answered."

"I apologize. They were probably rushing off to Wynantskill or Duanesburg."

"You said your sisters live there. Were you helping them?"

Her grin looked self-mocking. "My sisters helped me. Let's talk about something more fun. How're you and Luke doing?"

"We spend lots of free time on the yearbook. How's yours coming along?"

"Alice is an excellent editor-in-chief. I'm enjoying writing copy for some pages. She, I, and other Future Teachers of America kids visited an Albany State dorm on Western Avenue. Freshmen informally shared about college, including, 'Study, study, study! College is harder than high school.'"

Eva chuckled when I said, "Uh oh, a new worry: flunking out of college!"

Determined to avoid prying about her absence, I'm thankful that Eva seemed okay. Maybe she'll eventually confide more. She hates discussing diabetes.

Tuesday, March 13, 1962: Boxes

Hoping that 1,500 students would each buy a box of candy, we were speechless that 6,000 boxes were sold! Luke and I led the yearbook staff in applause for blushing Jake, who said, "Thank you."

I asked, "Jake, what are your sales secrets? How did you sell so many boxes?"

I giggled when he wisecracked, "I bought 3,000 myself... I'm sad that candy is missing from my doctor's diet. If we'd sold celery and carrot sticks, I'd be more irresistible."

I asked, "Did RPI's hockey season end positively?"

"Sixteen wins out of twenty-three games! In the quarterfinals of the league tournament last week, Colby College knocked RPI out of further play with a 7-6 win. In the tough Eastern College AC conference with twenty-eight teams, many strong, RPI ranked a respectable sixth."

"Maybe they'll go all the way once you're there! What kind of engineering will you major in?"

"Whatever's easiest!" I enjoy Jake's amusing modesty.

Saturday, March 17, 1962: AHS Boys' and Girls' Night

I'm pleased about the Albany newspaper photo of us Theta Alpha leaders after we won the Literary Bowl, modeled on the GE College Bowl TV quiz show! I was elated to have the most right answers to challenging questions English teachers devised about classic novels by the Brontes, Jane Austen, etc.

Hank, Udeh, Lon, and Marcus did a good job debating the National Forensic League topic: that the United States, for the good of its citizens, should withdraw from the United Nations. I can't imagine America quitting!

Monday, March 19, 1962: DAR

After AHS chose me as its female good citizen for demonstrating "dependability, leadership, service, and patriotism," I had to write a 300-word essay. The topic, *A Republic – If You Can Keep It*, was Ben Franklin's answer about the kind of government the Constitutional Convention created. I'm delighted that the DAR (Daughters of the American Revolution who must prove lineal descent from patriots of the Revolution) liked my essay enough to choose me as one of five Good Citizenship Award area winners.

Mom, uncertain about appropriate attire, seemed nervous when accompanying me to the Ten Broeck Mansion winners' tea. Wearing my gray wool suit with dark red bow blouse, I felt enthusiastic about my award.

Appreciating the honor and attired like DAR members in a black wool sheath with cultured pearls, I joined the other winners as DAR dinner guests at their Hotel Wellington meeting. The DAR reputation for bigotry made me grin wryly about two winners with immigrant grandparents: Schuyler's Italian-American Anna and me. The DAR would probably find an excuse to reject even a descendant of Haym Salomon, Jewish financier of the American Revolution.

Tuesday, March 20, 1962: Rival Veep

Working on the yearbook, I noticed something new: Luke and his veep holding hands in the large group FSE photo! Their arms are touching and both are beaming in the officers' photo! Taller and prettier than I with a curvier figure, his veep sings in the choir, is president of the Keyette charitable service group, and belongs to the National Honor Society, my literary society, and Forum. She won an NYS scholarship. Like other popular, fun girls who dated older boys now in college, she lacks a steady boyfriend. I can't blame Luke's going for her, especially if she's faster than I.

Coincidentally, Jim walked me home. "When will you get over your silly crush on Luke who has never been good enough for my *Osa Mamacita*?"

I laughed. "Why do you say that?"

"He's full of himself as a senior, worse than ever. Flirting outrageously with anyone wearing a skirt whenever you're not around, he must consider himself God's gift to womanhood."

I giggled. "Aren't you psychologically projecting?"

In front of my house, he chuckled. "I like that my *Osa Mamacita* has brains as well as beauty!" Caught off guard, I was quickly embraced and kissed full on the mouth. He ran off as I protested.

Wednesday, March 21, 1962: Flirting

Is Luke flirting because of my honors? I'm happier than ever as his girlfriend, confidante, and yearbook partner. Always a tastefully dressed gentleman, Luke is a model boyfriend and dance partner. If I'm his choice for dances, special events, and Saturday nights at movies and Mike's Log Cabin, I'll ignore anything he does with others. We aren't engaged or married. Though I've curbed all flirting since going steady, my incurable playfulness could come back at college.

Thursday, March 22, 1962: Newspapers

Craig teased me. "You've become so famous that friends are afraid to approach, but I'm not easily cowed. Only a week after your literary bowl photo appeared, your DAR award photo is in the Albany newspaper. Have you bewitched those hardened news photographers?" I giggled before he warmly congratulated me. I hope Luke doesn't feel threatened.

Saturday, March 24, 1962: Schuyler Concert

I phoned Eva who reported, "Bogged down in make-up schoolwork, I skipped the band concert."

"Are your parents impressed with your scholastic diligence?"

She snorted. "Satisfied without education, they don't care."

"You have so much ability, Eva! Isn't it unfair when girls can't fulfill their potential?"

"Of course! I want to be an attorney who helps women, Negroes, and other underprivileged people attain justice. The ruling class of rich white men will never voluntarily give up its privileges."

"Your acting, speaking, and writing talents will make you an excellent lawyer for underdogs!"

"Thank you. Do your parents favor college for girls?"

"After I saved both summers' job earnings, they've been supportive without pressuring me. Working days during the Depression, Dad felt bad about not graduating after years of evening college. I appreciate his weekly dollar in my college account."

"My family will deem me a success if I marry and produce kids. Without earning my keep, I'll be put up for adoption." I laughed at her joke. Since curiosity killed the cat, I said nothing but wished people were more like books in explaining mysteries.

Friday, March 30, 1962: Friday Thoughts

Instead of the usual fifty-degree March high, eighty degrees on my walk home was marvelous! I'm bubbly about spring's arrival!

Bless the synagogue's Mr. and Mrs. Club for including my parents in tonight's Sabbath service! Being at home alone without Mom's hostility is peaceful. I smiled cynically at the thought that Luke's petting or more with the FSE veep may have replaced Friday night Green Street prostitutes.

Saturday, March 31, 1962: Yearbook

At Mike's Log Cabin, Luke said, "Let's celebrate our baby being in the mail to the yearbook printer!"

I clinked my Singapore sling against his beer mug. "You must feel a huge a sense of accomplishment!"

He nodded. "You should, too! I couldn't have done it without you."

"Thank you, Luke! But you shouldered the responsibility. You made loads of decisions about every detail and ensured that more than forty kids did their jobs."

"Jake was great on sales. I didn't have to oversee him and the six sharp business staff kids. I was lucky to have you leading nine smart editors!"

"I appreciate that. Udeh took our best candid photos. Marcus and Marie worked hard on the activities and senior photos sections."

"So did you!" He grinned, looked into my eyes, put his arm around me, and kissed me on the lips. Then we danced to the Platters' great song, *Only You*, on the jukebox. He held me close and sang along with, "When you hold my hand, I understand the magic that you do." I felt loved and happy.

Sunday, April 1, 1962: Committees

Craig called. "Now that the yearbook's done, you belong to me. Tell Luke to get lost because I want you helping me oversee forty kids on senior committees every afternoon."

"Really? There's a lot left to do?"

"April fools' joke!" After I chuckled, he added, "Seriously, we're lucky that the dues committee collected enough money and that the ring committee selected, fit, ordered, and distributed rings which everyone seems to like."

"Luke included a photo of our hands wearing the rings in the yearbook."

"Good! The colors committee is creating four hundred ribbons for class day. I'm working with the committee on our class gift. I need you as a future psychologist to make sure no one's feelings are hurt by anything in the class will and class prophecy on class day."

"I'm glad to help. Craig, you're an outstanding president, especially leading kids so well!"

"Thank you! You're the best veep!" My heart's filled with fond feelings for Craig.

Saturday, April 7, 1962: Fabulous

Luke and I loved the movie musical *West Side Story* at the elegant Hellman. Identifying with Natalie Wood as Maria and feeling protected with Luke's arm around me, I sobbed about prejudice thwarting Tony's and Maria's love. "Stick to your own kind," from *A Boy Like That* sounded like my parents! I adored these songs: *Somewhere, Something's Coming, Maria, I Feel Pretty, Tonight,* and *One Hand One Heart.*

Monday, April 9, 1962: Oscars

Last night, I enjoyed the Oscar show with Luke's pleasant family. We applauded *West Side Story's* winning ten of eleven Oscars for which it was nominated, including best picture and best supporting actress, Rita Moreno! Luke and I cheered when *Splendor in the Grass* won best original screenplay!

Since the great *Breakfast at Tiffany's* song *Moon River* got an Oscar, I've pictured the Hudson River flowing down to NYC and sung, "I'm crossing you in style someday...Wherever you're going, I'm going your way."

Friday, April 13, 1962: Winter

So much for spring! Is Friday the Thirteenth making mischief again with over three inches of snow? I hope that it's gone by Easter vacation next week. Dear Diary, do you like my Japanese-style tanka nature poem in 5-7-5-7-7 format?

> *Albany Winter*
> Gray skies months on end
> Dirty snow hiding sidewalks
> Prancing down the street
> We slip and fall on sly ice
> Concealed by recent blizzards

Saturday, April 14, 1962: Spring Frolic

Thank you, Mr. and Mrs. Club and Bruce Bilder's Continentals, for keeping the parents out late dancing. Returning from Mike's Log Cabin, Luke and I relished making out on the couch without the usual vigilance about pulling apart should Dad, puttering around in the back of our flat, approach.

Friday, April 20, 1962: Wilde

After finishing *The Picture of Dorian Gray* for English class, I enjoyed witty Oscar Wilde's *The Ideal Husband*. I giggled at lines like, "Fashion is what one wears oneself. What is unfashionable is what other people wear," "Morality is the attitude we adopt towards those we personally dislike," "Life is never fair and it's a good thing for most of us," and "If we men married the women we deserved, we should have a very bad time." These 1895 Wilde lines, however, are depressing: "A woman who can keep a man's love and love him in return has done all the world wants of women or should want of them," and "A man's life is of more value than a woman's."

Sunday, April 22, 1962: Easter

Since vacation began Wednesday, my mood has been cheerful! Today, Dad drove us to Gloversville. Though it rained, I welcomed the summery temperature. Ella was at the JCC for an art group meeting. Lydia described the sweetheart ball: "I had a wonderful time with a cute Italian senior who's a great dancer! I met him in glee club where he solos. His tenor voice romantically serenaded me as we slow danced."

"Fabulous! I'm glad that you're dating anyone you want!"

"Since my date with the Negro basketball star, Ella has helped me get around the parents. I've flirted with a couple of possible junior and senior prom dates!"

"I'll never forgive my parents for keeping me from dating the triumvirate during sophomore and junior years. With musketeers Craig, Dominic, and Jake, I could have enjoyed four big dances and proms I missed! If other boys had known that I could date gentiles, I might have gone to the other two proms."

I agreed when Lydia said, "Nothing's meaner to a teen girl than keeping her from big dances!"

Monday, April 23, 1962: Doreen

Vacation is marvelous. Though not in the eighties like yesterday, today was warm enough to walk to Stewart's for ice cream. While I enjoyed rum raisin, Doreen spooned up strawberry and said, "I'm in a great mood after a wonderful weekend in Springfield at Logan's lovely Victorian-style home. His parents are extremely nice!"

"I'm glad! How do you feel about Logan?"

"I like him more than any boy I've known. He's smart, good-looking, and fun with a great future as an engineer. But I'm too young to know if he's *The One*. He wants us to be together next year in Boston after he transfers. I'll miss him because I can't afford a private, out-of-state college."

"He must be in love. I feel too young to know about the future, too...If you had the money, would you go to Boston?"

"Sure. It beats Buffalo!"

Wednesday, April 25, 1962: Scholarships

College acceptance has helped me relax on vacation! I've loved sleeping late and lazy-daisying around without something to do every minute. Thanks to Dad's low income, Barnard and Binghamton's Harpur College, my second choice, provided scholarships. My NYS scholarship will help me afford Barnard.

I congratulated Luke on his $500 University of Rochester scholarship and Craig on $700 of Hamilton College financial aid when they called!

Thursday, April 26, 1962: Mom

Mom said that her busy occupational therapy boss, Mrs. Viola McGrath, kindly took time to write:

> Fern, you did a beautiful job of typing and making attractive the cover letter and chart by Mr. Z to Jacques Cattrell Press. I'm filing a copy of this note in your personnel file.

While Dad said, "Hon, it's good that you're appreciated at work and home," I mischievously wished that Mom's boss would put this memo in her file:

> Fern, your critical attitude towards your daughter must improve immediately to avoid demerits, pay reduction, and job termination!

Tuesday, May 1, 1962: Spring

I adore daylight savings time! I'm sure that Albany's Tulip Queen finalists, to be announced tomorrow, also vote against May snow!

Friday, May 4, 1962: Student Day

Poised debater and student council veep Udeh excelled as MC of today's role-switching program. President Craig was vice-principal for the day. I was lucky to be guidance counselor, similar to psychologist and natural and fun for me. A student rating committee evaluated the performance of students elected to teach for the day in every class. I felt more respect for our teachers who make it look easy. After juniors like Jim were inducted into the National Honor Society, I appreciated my *Excellence in Extracurricular Activities* award from the student council.

Saturday, May 5, 1962: Play

When I called, Eva said, "Our zany school play, *You Can't Take It With You*, was a hit yesterday. As the understudy who helped with publicity, I laughed at the hilarious lines."

"Which part would you like to play?"

"Of the juicy female roles, I'll take the klutzy daughter who takes ballet lessons and is married to Paul!" After I giggled, she added, "Though her sister, the romantic lead, has more lines, their eccentric mother who writes sexy melodramas and paints pictures is funnier. Anna as the visiting actress who gets drunk and Alice as the Russian grand duchess and friend of the ballet teacher had good lines... Angela, what's up?"

"For Student Day, English classmates picked me to bore them for almost an hour and prove that I'd be even worse at teaching than you consider yourself at sports." She chuckled before I asked, "Besides Paul, were any cute guys in the play?"

"My former date John played the eccentric father. Keith, whom I'm now seeing, played a G-man. Only slightly younger than I, Keith's an attractive, smart junior with plans to be a doctor, unique for Schuyler." We both laughed.

"He sounds great for the senior prom!"

Sunday, May 6, 1962: Birthday

On a pleasant Gloversville day, I said to Ella, "At thirteen, you seem more like a high school student!" My family gave her a silver *Ella* charm. Sharing chocolate birthday cake, I enjoyed feeling like a sister: Lydia, Ella, and I wore gold initial rings from Grandma.

Wednesday, May 9, 1962: Don Juan

Jim continues to flirt and walk me home. "If you come to your senses soon and dump Luke, we'll have a blast at our proms! Luke's flirting is increasingly outrageous."

I smiled. "Doesn't it take one to know one?"

Grinning, Jim took my hand. "Sweet *Osa Mamacita*, stop being loyal to that cheater. Be my junior prom date May 19!" Since Jim rarely tries for physical contact, today's buss on the lips caught me by surprise. Though it felt good, I pitied his girlfriend at St. Agnes. Does she realize he's a Don Juan? Paul's Catholic school girlfriends don't see him with his Schuyler fans.

Saturday, May 12, 1962: Tulip Festival

On a cool day, Luke and I enjoyed seeing pretty Nancy Self, age twenty-one, crowned Tulip Queen in Washington Park! As we strolled among the colorful tulip beds, I was interested to hear, "Angela, I read that World War II prevented Albany's first festival in 1940 from being repeated until *Knickerbocker News* City Editor Charles Mooney's 1948 column inspired the 1949 festival." Because tickets are so expensive, I was lucky to attend the 1961 Tulip Ball.

Sunday, May 13, 1962: Mom's Day

After I gave Mom breakfast in bed and a handmade card, Dad asked, "Hon, would you like to celebrate Mother's Day at the Tulip Festival band concert?"

My eyebrows went up in surprise after she answered, "Let's estimate Barnard expenses so I can stop worrying about whether we have enough money." Wondering why there's doubt, I feared Mom's sabotaging my plans. Grandpa's last-minute cruelty, stopping her from attending Syracuse University because of bedpans, after she had packed her student nursing uniforms, made me feel sick about history repeating itself.

Sitting around our charcoal gray Formica and wrought iron dinette table, we listed $2,800 of freshman expenses: tuition, dorm, and fees $2,266; books and supplies $85; clothes $150; travel home $50; $5-per-week allowance $250. Mom said, "Your NYS summer job should bring in $615. The NYS scholarship and new scholar incentive total $1,000. The Barnard scholarship is $325."

Dad said, "Your college savings account has around $1,500. We should be okay for the first year."

I breathed a sigh of relief. "Dad, thanks for saving since I was born!" Dad looked pleased and Mom's expression softened.

At the Albany Institute of History and Art, the unusual varieties of tulips and floral arrangements were beautiful. My favorites were purple, pink, and variegated. I was surprised that tulips arrived in Europe from Turkey in 1560 and the Dutch had a 400th anniversary flower show in 1960.

After my parents and I saw *All Fall Down*, I grinned about the movie's son, played by cute Warren Beatty, behaving badly enough for perfectionist Mom to realize that I could be worse.

I prayed to God to help Eva and me graduate from college.

Friday, May 18, 1962: Schuyler Choir

After a pleasant sunny day in the nineties, I enjoyed hearing kids I know sing music favorites! Schuy-Larks, ten girls with the best voices, sang *I Feel Pretty* from *West Side Story* and four more songs. An opera aria from Puccini's *Madame Butterfly* highlighted soloist Alice's lovely voice! She also narrated *Simon, The Fisherman*. Anna's solos reminded me of an opera singer! The program listed both as future music majors, Anna at NYS Teachers' College at Fredonia and Alice at Albany's Saint Rose College.

Tenor soloist Ric, looking cuter than ever, did well singing a Christian hymn: *Somebody's Knocking at Your Door*. Did the *Exodus* theme song help the one Jewish boy in the choir feel better about performing four Christian songs mentioning Jesus at a public school? Remembering the Holocaust with tears in my eyes, I've been singing *Exodus'* moving lyrics, "I see a land where children can run free," and "I'll fight to make this land our own. Until I die, this land is mine."

I congratulated alto Eva afterwards. "Eva, I loved hearing favorites like *Begin the Beguine, Once in Love with Amy, Thumbelina,* and *You Are Beautiful.* I often play our *Flower Drum Song* album to hear *I Enjoy Being a Girl, Love Look Away,* and *Grant Avenue.*"

"Rodgers and Hammerstein music is outstanding!"

"Why do you think Schuyler's concerts seem better than AHS's?"

"Our music teachers are so dedicated that numerous kids join and work hard." Eva added that her boyfriend Keith is a bass in the choir.

I responded, "Deep voices thrill me."

"They are sexy! Keith left to help his grandparents or I would have introduced you." I wondered whether Luke was with his FSE veep.

Sunday, May 20, 1962: Anna's

I phoned Eva. "Have you had a fun weekend?"

"Last night, Keith and I enjoyed Anna's party for choir members at her home on your former Morton Avenue. Keith helped this klutz dance better than usual, especially to *Three Stars Will Shine Tonight.*"

"How does it go?"

"It's from TV's Dr. Kildare." She sang, "And for the third star, only one reason, a star you can wish on to make dreams come true."

"That sounds romantic!"

"Keith's a good influence, wanting me to quit smoking, like my doctor. Unfortunately, I'm addicted. How has your weekend been?"

"I love this weather! Yesterday when it was over ninety, Luke was sweet to drive me to the Helderbergs. After swimming at Thacher, we took the back roads and found an unspoiled, quaint village called Rensselaerville. The cemetery has grave stones going back to the eighteenth century! The waterfall is romantic."

"I'll ask Keith to take me there!"

Monday, May 21, 1962: Lilacs

I love the color and fragrance of our backyard lilac bush in bloom! If only we could reach the flowers twenty feet up...

Saturday, May 26, 1962: Awards

Dad, holding the newspaper, said, "We just had thirteen consecutive days with warmer-than-average high temperatures."

"Herm, it's about time after thirty-five inches of February snow, three times the norm and the most since 1893!" I had to agree with Mom.

Before evening dates with our boyfriends, Eva and I enjoyed the remaining Washington Park tulips. I was interested to hear about Schuyler's recognition day yesterday. "Paul got an art award. Alice got a choral music key, the top award. Choral music pins went to Ric, Jennie, and Anna, who also got a bowling prize."

"Does Ric still carry a torch for Jennie?"

"He's pining because she's moved on to other boys."

I asked, "Did you get an acting key?"

"How did you know?"

"Because you're talented!"

"Thank you, Angela! One of the Johns I dated got an acting pin. Alice deserved her yearbook key and Red Cross award. I was lucky to receive a yearbook pin. Schuyler gives points for extracurricular activities. Fourteen seniors with the greatest number of points got awards, including Alice, Paul, Anna, Ric, a John I dated, and yours truly. At graduation, Paul or a John will be the winning male citizen. The top female citizen will be Anna or Alice."

"How about you, Eva?"

"Too many teachers know I'm irreverent!" While laughing, I wondered whether Eva's absence prevented her top citizen nomination and why she was gone so long.

Sunday, May 27, 1962: Sex

Eva and I met at the Delaware to see *A Taste of Honey*, a touching English movie about a plain girl our age, played by Rita Tushingham. A Negro sailor left her pregnant. Afterwards, my eyes kept watering. "I'm sad about girls with broken hearts getting stuck raising kids alone."

"Guys definitely take advantage. They lie about love and promise anything to get sex. Afterwards, they're gone without the tender emotions we feel."

I wondered whether a boyfriend lied to and abandoned Eva. "Eva, how do we make things fairer for girls?"

"Fathers should oil their shotguns!"

I cracked up before Eva said more seriously, "Rita, whose mother loved the bottle more than her, was forlorn without male protectors."

"I'm glad to be with Luke who respects my limits and gets enough allowance for Green Street."

"Do the boys have sex with prostitutes?"

"Years ago, Luke mentioned it, along with Gayety Music Hall burlesque shows."

"Do the women strip?"

"They dance around and act risqué in some way. I've avoided those topics this year."

"Who wants the sordid details?" We giggled.

Thursday, June 1, 1962: Class Night

Today's fourth and final school newspaper edition shows us officers in front of our fabulous senior class gift: a huge garnet sign with *Albany Senior High School* in light gray letters near AHS on Western Avenue. A plaque on the stainless steel frame reads *Gift: Class of 1962*. We're excited to sponsor an important contribution which should last many years.

The AHS orchestra played as we seniors, adorned with blue and silver class ribbons, marched into the school auditorium. I was impressed with Luke's speech about our Garnet and Gray yearbook dedicatee. Popular Coach Sutin has taught at AHS for almost twice as long as we've been alive! Our class poet's verses, which will appear in the yearbook, sounded ideal!

Julia was one of six teens driving to a fun spring picnic adventure in the one-act class play, *Antic Spring* by Robert Nail. Neal presented the class will and class prophecy. Our class songwriter led us in singing her touching creation.

We laughed often and cried sentimental tears listening to President Craig's speech, a triumph! I smiled picturing Craig and me as parents of our class...the only parents with 400 offspring. Class Night was perfect!

Saturday, June 2, 1962: Senior of the Issue

On the kitchen floor, I deliberately dropped a school newspaper copy opened to Marcus' photo. I could barely keep a straight face when Mom found it, as intended. At dinner, she predictably said, "Marcus is a National Merit Scholarship finalist and a finalist twice in the United Nations contest."

I answered, "I have yet to hear of that contest. Maybe he made it up."

Dropping her objection after noticing that I controlled a giggle, Mom said, "He'll be at Columbia, across the street from Barnard!"

I laughed. "So will Udeh." One of the most persistent people on earth, Mom looked to heaven before I escaped to my room.

Monday, June 4, 1962: Mista

Our exchange student, always smiling, fun, and modest, is a favorite classmate. Tears came to my eyes after we exchanged senior photos and I read her words on the back:

Dearest Angela, the girl in AHS that means the most to me. I'm so proud to be your friend and so thankful to have met you. I admire you so much (I think you know by now?) and it will be so sad not to see you anymore. You are the most wonderful person I know and I will miss you very much. I'm happy and thankful for the good time we've had together and hope we will meet again. Any time I can help you, I will be glad to. My home is always open to you. Please try to come to Norway. I wish you the very best of luck. Love always, Mista

Since she's popular with lots of friends, I had no idea that she considered me special. I'll miss her.

Tuesday, June 5, 1962: Baby Bear

Walking me home, Jim requested a signed copy of my senior photo. His comment on the large color version of his picture showed his playful imagination: "To my mama bear, don't ever forget baby bear and all his friends (Tumba) because he will always cherish your memory. May we always have what we have now. A motto: we have nothing to fear but fear itself. Always, Jim." With a steady girlfriend, he must consider our bantering friendship enough.

Jim

Wednesday, June 6, 1962: Cara

When Cara and I exchanged senior photos, I wrote:

> Dear Cara, Your photo looks great! I will always remember our special talks during walks to Hackett. Your company made shivering to death in the winter bearable. As a math whiz with a wonderful personality and high grades in all subjects, you will have a successful future. I will miss you and our friendship! Love, Angela

I appreciated everything she wrote:

> Dear Angela, for four years, we have studied and had fun together. I could never ask for a truer friend than you've been. I have always been able to tell you my troubles and I have gladly listened also. Your friendship and understanding I will always remember. I hope the end of high school doesn't end our friendship. That would be a great loss. I hope that we will be able to see each other frequently in the future. In four years I will be thrilled when I hear that you are valedictorian of Barnard. Good luck, love, and fun in all you do. Remember always! Love, Cara

Friday, June 8, 1962: Schuyler

At Schuyler's annual Senior Class Prize Speaking and Class Night, Craig and I enjoyed watching Eva perform an excerpt from *The Nun's Story*! I loved Audrey Hepburn in this movie!

Eva's *Stanley* presented *The Challenge of the Ages* before Anna gave a *Pygmalion* reading. Alice's *Mary of Scotland* reading was excellent!

I was entranced when Ric sang a favorite romantic *Camelot* song: *If Ever I Would Leave You*. From the quiet boy who went to the movies with Eva, Xavier, and me in 1959, he has grown up into an even better-looking, confident young man.

Poised MC Paul's speech about *My Responsibilities as an American Citizen* reminded me that he lived in Sicily until age four.

Editor Alice presented the terrific yearbook! One of the many Johns gave the class log. *Stanley* presented the prophecy. Anna got laughs reading the class will. Eva's rendition of her excellent class poem was moving.

Complimenting Eva and others, I got autographs from her and Ric. To Paul, I said, "Will a future movie star like you please autograph my program?" Captivated by his smile, I beamed as he signed.

Seeing Xavier with his pretty girlfriend, Eva whispered, "Despite being knocked down, she's still with him. Can you believe that he skipped applying to colleges?"

Shocked, I murmured, "What a waste of brains! Albany State would be free with his NYS scholarship."

Sunday, June 10, 1962: New Cousins

An exciting NYC day featured Cousin Hal's marriage! As a hopeless romantic, I adore weddings! Seeing the love in Hal's eyes as he looked down at Eileen brought tears. I hope that someday the man I marry will look at me that way.

Eileen's congratulations about my Barnard acceptance made me happy. I can't wait for her upcoming college guide, *Questions Freshmen Ask*!

During the lively reception, Dad's cousin's wife said, "With my husband and three sons at home, I miss female company. Come see us on Long Island this summer, Angela. We're near Jones Beach." After hitting it off with her oldest son Adam, I'm eager to visit. Still in high school, tall Adam's an athletic top student with a fun, magnetic personality. Being the only girl my age was a blast with Adam or college student sons of Dad's other cousins partnering me for every dance!

Hal & Eileen

Handsome cousin Adam

Sunday, June 17, 1962: Dad's Day

Dad laughed at the card I made:

> Happy Father's Day to the sweetest, nicest, kindest, most intelligent, most lovable, cutest, most amusing, most wonderful father .... I have!
>
> Love, Your Nicest Daughter

Dad's choice of a steak dinner by mediocre cooks Mom and me over a restaurant meal seemed idiotic. Canasta afterwards was fun.

Luke described a similar celebration. Is poor Luke again playing *second fiddle* with his brother home from NYU?

Tuesday, June 19, 1962: Chicken

Though I want Sara at my graduation, I'm too chicken to rock the boat with my parents by calling her. Though I mailed her birthday card with my graduation date, time, and place, I'm not holding my breath for a miracle.

Thursday, June 21, 1962: They

Done with exams, I was celebrating adored summer days until Mom said, "Angela, the girls in the steno pool asked whether you'll be out all night after the prom. When I answered, 'Of course not,' they looked surprised. When will you return home?"

"Everyone goes to Lake George, stays up all night, watches the sunrise, and swims on Sunday."

"What will they think about your reputation?"

"Who are *they*?"

"Friends and neighbors."

"Everyone will be together doing the same thing." Does she really expect me to skip something I want because some neighbor I hardly know will disapprove? I can't wait to escape from the pressure to conform to avoid negative Albany gossip.

Friday, June 22, 1962: Romeos

Last night's dream, without my usual nervousness about something like a test, was enchanting: at Barnard, I double-dated with Sara to see *Romeo and Juliet* at the Metropolitan Opera. Celebrating her forty-fifth birthday, she was with a charming, attentive gentleman her age. I was with an attractive Columbia guy, someone passionate about music like Dominic.

Saturday, June 23, 1962: Senior Ball

The beauty parlor set, teased, and sprayed my limp, shoulder-length, straight hair to last overnight! The longer it grows, the better it looks. Luke surprised me with a gorgeous bouquet of white and red roses! He looked handsome in his white dinner jacket, bow tie, and dark trousers. At the Aurania Club, *Remember When* was a perfect prom theme. Three hours of dancing to Pete Emma's Orchestra and talking to numerous classmates whizzed by. Though most girls wore unwieldy full-length formals, I was cool and comfortable in my simple silky dress with spaghetti straps. After staying up to enjoy a lovely sunrise, we swam at Lake George today. Unlike the 1961 prom with a boy I hardly knew, this dance with Luke was the perfect celebration of a magnificent year together.

Prom

Sunday, June 24, 1962: Rest

Eva shared about the Schuyler prom. "Paul's date was a pretty parochial school girl. Ric took a junior with a fun sense of humor...After last winter's nightmare, I'm thankful for prom fun with Keith. I'm sorry that I was out of touch so long. Waiting on me during bed rest was hard on my family, especially my pregnant older sister with a mischievous toddler. So I moved to the house of my second sister, tired during her first pregnancy. After cleaning all day, Mother drove through bad weather to care for me evenings and weekends to give my sisters time with their husbands. Dad's medical problems made him ignore the phone. My parents were too overwhelmed to remember who called or write down messages. Thanks again for your cards which I found after returning home in late February."

"Thanks for explaining. I missed you and was afraid that you were in the hospital."

"The hospital would have been easier, but was beyond our budget. I'm lucky not to be returned for a refund or exchanged for a healthier daughter," she joked.

I laughed. "I love your sense of humor! Were you bored?"

"No one had time to get library books. I devoured everything I found, mainly magazines and newspapers. I was desperate enough to read my chemist brother-in-law's textbooks, technical books, and journals." We chuckled.

"I'm happy that you're better! I'll stay mum." Eva's confiding rewarded my patience in avoiding questions. I'm sorry that she was isolated from friends during a possibly life-threatening crisis. She must have been frightened. I feel honored to be trusted. The information feels like a gift because she hates discussing medical stuff. Dear Diary, you're the only one I'm telling. Will I ever learn why Eva needed bed rest?

Monday, June 25, 1962: *Garnet and Gray*

I'm thankful for my final exam grades: English 97, chemistry 98, typing 98, and, despite *Bs* all semester, advanced algebra 93.

After we got our yearbooks, I felt a warm glow reading, "It is just the greatest yearbook ever! Love, Rex"

Jake blushed while thanking me after I said, "Your fundraising leadership enabled us to pay for the yearbook improvements. I'm impressed that you helped AHS succeed as baseball team catcher! Congratulations on your $1,400 RPI scholarship!"

Luke nodded after I said, "The kids' yearbook compliments make me feel rewarded." With his arm around me, he squeezed my shoulder after I added: "You deserve credit for innovation: expanding to 200 pages; adding ruby, emerald, and sapphire duo-tone color photo pages; increasing senior photo size and decreasing to seven per page; using candid rather than formal faculty photos; giving seniors padded tricolor covers with gold engraved names; and including seventy-two candid shots, some with unusual shapes and angles!"

Compliments about the foreword I wrote were gratifying. Our yearbook's theme is *Forward*. Each italicized category below corresponds to a yearbook section:

FORWARD

We of the Class of 1962 are graduating from Albany High School which, especially in the senior year, has provided us with the challenges and experiences necessary for us to go FORWARD successfully into the adult world. We have had devoted *faculty* to guide us, *senior class* officers to lead us, *academic courses* to challenge us, *social activities* to entertain us, *extracurricular organizations* to unify us, team *sports* to strengthen us, respectful *underclassmen* to follow us, and helpful *businessmen* to aid us. This yearbook, the 1962 GARNET AND GRAY, will serve as a record of our senior year and the last steps we have taken before going FORWARD into society.

Tuesday, June 26, 1962: Schuyler Graduation

I missed seeing Eva and 142 classmates graduate because family members used all the tickets. Near Washington Park's perfumed roses, Eva said, "Our commencement address annoyed Xavier, Ric, and me. A local attorney labeled unconstitutional the recent Supreme Court decision banning mandatory prayer in public schools. Distorting the Declaration of Independence reference to a creator, this lawyer would have felt threatened by and called communist a deist like Thomas Jefferson. What happened to freedom of religion and separation of church and state?"

I responded, "Narrow Albany minds are scary...Who got graduation prizes?"

"Alice deserved and got the foreign language prize, the Italian prize, and the Business and Professional Women's Club scholarship. Paul won for best class night oration. Xavier won the Sears Foundation Award."

"What's that for?"

"Being the most girlfriend-beating, irreverent senior."

I guffawed before asking, "Did you win anything?"

"Knights of Pythias English prize, graduation essay prize, and poetry award."

"Congratulations, Eva! What are your plans?"

"Hoping my parents relent about charging me rent, I'll attend St. Rose until my savings run out."

"You're the most brilliant girl I've ever met! You deserve to finish college more than anyone. If my parents didn't need to rent out our spare room, you could live there free. You're a wonderful friend! Is there any way I can help?"

Tears were in her eyes as she shook her head no. "Thanks for the supportive words and loyal friendship!" We parted after a hug.

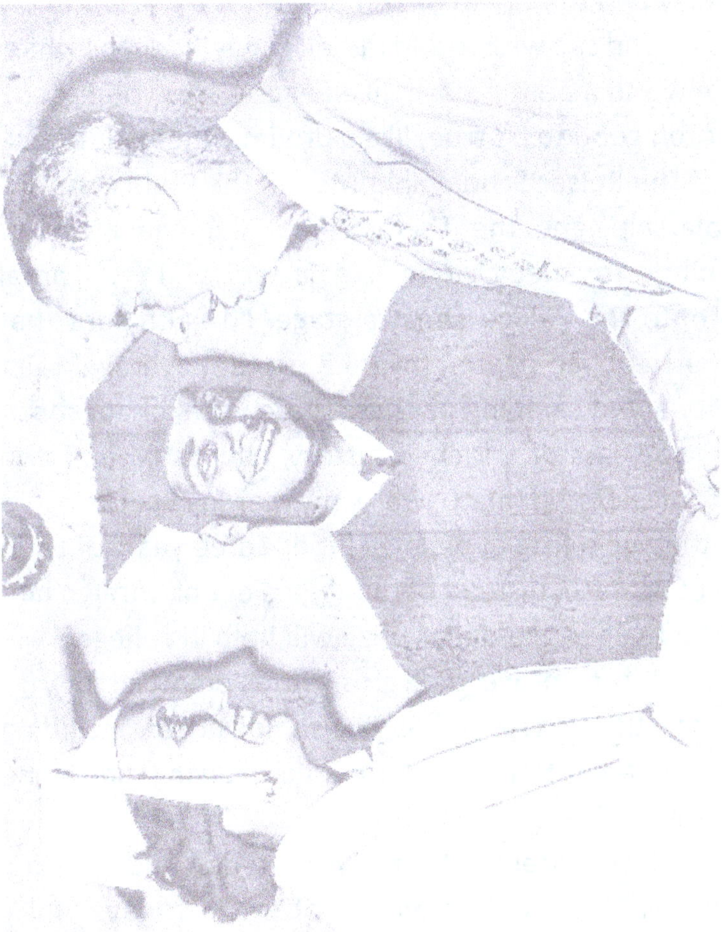

Alice & Ric

Wednesday, June 27, 1962: Bittersweet Day

Commencement speaker Dr. Holmes told us 399 graduates, "You're lucky to be young in the most exciting era the world has ever seen," and urged us "to strengthen democracy in this country and to help to pass it around the world." In my white gown and cap with a gold tassel, I imagined jobs which make the world a better place, like Peace Corps volunteer.

It felt too good to be true, like a dream, when our principal said, "The Belser Scholarship Medal, the Pythias Award for Scholarship, and the Theta Sigma Alumnae Prize for English all go to valedictorian Angela Weiss." I felt unreal walking onto the Palace Theatre stage. I'd been sure that Marcus or Neal had beaten my 96.7 percent average. I felt a bit guilty about skipping physics. Three years of advanced English, two years of enriched history, chemistry, and two years of accelerated math were my hardest courses. To avoid cutting up a frog in biology, I took three years of Latin and two of Spanish, instead of four years of one foreign language. The twenty-five-dollar prize will help in college.

Determined to prove that girls are as smart as boys, I was pleased that girls won half the senior prizes, including Julia for dramatics, Henrietta for public speaking, and Irene for an essay.

Glad that my parents, Aunt Myrna, Lydia, and Ella saw me graduate, I missed Sara on one of the best days of my life. I feel honored to continue as lifetime class veep.

Aware that I'll soon be a small, unknown fish in the big NYC sea, I went around AHS thanking my dedicated teachers and saying goodbye to wonderful classmates. My heart overflowed with love. Though elated about graduating first,

I'm sad to leave so many caring people. Sentimental tears brimmed over for hours. After we go our separate ways in life, I doubt we seniors can recapture the precious closeness we now enjoy. With eyes still red, I'm grieving about today's loving feelings gradually fading.

With Ella & Lydia

Thursday, June 28, 1962: Court

The Supreme Court ruling about no mandatory public school prayers represents progress. I've always been uncomfortable about prayers mentioning Jesus and Christ forced on me because Christians are the majority.

All for muscular male bodies, including sculptures, I'm gleeful about the Supreme Court decision that nude male photos are no longer obscene. Why did Marcus' cousin's yearbook note about our running joke come to mind? "Dear Angela, you are a very sweet, humble, and lovely girl. I wish you the best of luck in your future life. If I become an Italian movie star, I will ask you to play the leading role with me."

Friday, June 29, 1962: Party

Doreen's graduation party was heartwarming! Everyone brought yearbooks! Luke and I enjoyed signing them and dancing to hit records.

I grinned reading my old nickname: "Dear Ajax, You're the girl who deserves the best of everything. I'm sure therefore that with your charm and personality, you'll succeed in everything you do. Please keep in touch. Love, Tara." She'll follow in her sister's footsteps, studying to be a social worker at Syracuse University!

Referring to *most likely to succeed*, Udeh said, "I'm honored to be your co-winner in the senior favorites poll." I felt touched reading his words: "You've been a shining light in my eyes for four wonderful years. I shall never forget your tremendous charm, personality, and perseverance. I'm looking forward to the next four years together at Columbia. With love and admiration, Udeh."

My eyes were watery reading Bea's comments: "We'll all be going our separate ways. When you're in your nineties and read this book, never forget the girl from Colonie Central High. Remember our great times at Hebrew School and in fifth grade, including the tents we built in my old house. Remember me as I will never forget you!"

I smiled at my husband Tad after he wrote, "Our friendship has been and I hope always shall be a marvelous one. Don't forget our long and dear marriage. May you live all you want and not want all you live. Love!"

I hugged Doreen who wrote: "I hope you know how fond I am of you. We've grown up together and I've loved every minute. You don't know how happy I am that you're here (my party). You deserve the very best life can offer. Stay as sweet and nice and sincere as you are. Love always!" Doreen confided, "When Marsha and I are at Buffalo State, I'll miss Logan."

I responded, "I understand. Do you feel any interest in meeting new boys?"

"I guess so. I'm looking forward to living in a new place, but afraid of even worse winters." Thankful to be going south, I nodded sympathetically. Doreen asked, "How did you get a summer job? I need work but there are 200 applicants for every state summer job."

"I got interviewed because my mother knows the NYS Insurance Department clerical supervisor, who asked about my grades and warned that filing insurance forms all summer is boring. I answered, 'I need money for college and will be grateful for any state job.' Today was my second day. Everyone's nice. It pays well: over $1.50 an hour! After such an exhilarating, hectic year, I'm relieved to let my mind drift while I file. Doreen, do you still plan to teach?"

"It's my dream job."

"My mother, who wants me to teach, would prefer you as a daughter! Your students will be lucky to have a kind, conscientious, dedicated instructor!"

"Thanks, Angela! You'll be a good psychologist. You've always listened to my feelings and been helpful!"

"Thank you! People fascinate me. I'd like to help them lead happier lives. You'll inspire your students to be the best citizens."

Saturday, June 30, 1962: Reactions

Mom said, "Marcus won two English graduation prizes. If you weren't with Luke, he might've invited you to the prom. You look best with a tall, blond, blue-eyed boy like Marcus."

"My interest in Marcus is platonic."

"He must go for you after escorting you to a Blue Moon and the sixth-grade Boy Scout dance. What did he write in your yearbook?"

"To a swell kid, Angela. Hoping you have lots of educated success at Barnard. I'm sure you will. Luv, Marcus"

"See," Mom said, "he wrote *love*."

"*L u v* means *like*." Mom should appreciate my agreeable Jewish boyfriend, who masterminded a wonderful yearbook. Luke and I have yet to sign each other's books, maybe because the entire book is like our child, a treasured gift to each other.

Mom said, "Herm, my brother Peter called about the Gloversville newspaper article Abner wrote about Angela as valedictorian and scholarship recipient. I'm mentioned as the sister of Abner and Peter Cline. Peter, who mailed the article, said, 'We're proud of Angela. She can pick out college clothes from my store as a graduation gift.'" I'm eager for new clothes!

Dad asked, "Are things better since Peter and Abner divided your father's corporation in 1959?"

Mom answered, "Yes. Peter enjoys Best Wholesale. Abner prefers Cline's Department Store."

Uncle Peter

Sunday, July 1, 1962: Reminiscing

Feeling fortunate to be appreciated at school, I finally found time for more than a quick glance at about a hundred year-book entries from classmates and teachers. Reading them was comforting when I felt let down about high school ending. I copied the following precious words from dear female friends to preserve in case my yearbook gets lost.

Our beautiful Blue Moon queen, Irene, voted *most popular*, wrote: "You're really headed for a wonderful life and you deserve it. *Did most for the school* and *most likely to succeed* are both understatements. You're the pride and joy of the class of 1962. God was good to you. He gave you beauty and brains both. I know you'll have a great time at Barnard. Tell my Aunt Helen (Barnard official) to take good care of you. Always keep in touch. May your every wish come true. Love!"

I value my friendship with class secretary Henrietta, voted *most versatile* girl, who wrote: "I shall never forget you. It has really been a pleasure and experience for me to have known and worked with you at AHS. I am sure that you will succeed in whatever you attempt. May God ever bless you. Love!"

I smiled reading Julia's words: "You've been such a wonderful friend these last years that I'll never forget you. Please stay as sweet, modest, and unassuming as you are now. I'll never forget the English and Latin courses we took together or the homeroom periods we spent talking. One last Mooooo! Love!"

I couldn't be happier than to receive love and warm wishes from girls whose image of me is a sweet friend who has helped our school.

Monday, July 2, 1962: Card

After walking through Washington Park to work on Lark Street, I mailed a congratulations card to Alice who deserved and won a huge honor: NYS Volunteer of the Year!

Card to Alice

Tuesday, July 3, 1962: Precious Words

After work, I copied more special yearbook comments.

Unsentimental Hank wrote: "In view of your former accomplishment, I shall overlook your academic career except to wish you continued success. However, all the books and vicarious experience of teachers are useless without *primary experience*. Life is for living and it is precious short. My advice to you is *live it*. If you do, as I hope, you will undoubtedly mature into an exceptional woman in all ways." I've been more socially active than he, so what does *live it* mean? I hope it's not losing virginity. Don't males realize girls' futures can be ruined?

The message of a smart, handsome Protestant boy I've admired but who didn't pursue me astonished and thrilled me: "Don't ever forget the good times in advanced algebra and solid geometry. I'm getting all misty when I think of how sweet you were to me. You were and still are a *Doll*! You were always so sweet and lovable. I'm only sorry I didn't get to know you earlier. This is an honor for me to write in *Your Book*! I could go on forever. You made my days at AHS a pleasure. You did more for everyone's morale than anyone else. You are my people. I will always love you. Love, love, love!"

In intelligent, good-looking Lee's book, I expressed affectionate feelings. It was heartwarming to ogle his barechested wrestling team yearbook photo and read: "To the sweetest girl of the class of 1962: I hope the future brings happiness and good luck. Always remember me for I will always remember your pleasant smiles and your sweetness at all times. I just want you to know that I felt the same way about you. Love always!"

Wednesday, July 4, 1962: Precious Continued

Off work, I copied yearbook comments from boys I'll always love.

I feel that Jake's succinct message is from the heart: "Dearest Angela, I'll never forget you and the times we've had. I hope we see each other often. Love!"

I treasure Dominic's words: "My dearest Angela, roses are red, my love; violets are blue; sugar is sweet, my love; but not as sweet as you. You I'll never forget. I hope you remember me and everything we did together. I wish you the best of luck at Barnard and the rest of your life. Love always!"

Tears overflowed as I read Craig's words: "Angela, my one and only, you know you're the only girl for me. I'll wait for you until you get over that silly infatuation with Luke. These four years have been out of this world because of you. You were my ego-builder when I was low. You laughed at my jokes and liked my singing. You were my right hand this whole year. My success is your success. You can't win enough prizes to suit me. I love you, always will, and always have. Your senior class president." I'll miss the *most versatile* boy and his hilarious jokes. Adoring him, I hope to stay in touch.

Thursday, July 5, 1962: Mr. V

Do my parents see Mr. V to improve their marriage or only to get a rebel offspring to toe the line as a Jewish conformist? At their request, I visited Mr. V. I showed my yearbook as evidence against Mom's criticisms. After reading friends' remarks, Mr. V said, "Thanks for sharing. Why do you think that you're popular at school?"

"I'm sad when snobbism hurts kids so I've gone out of my way to smile, say hi, and be friendly to everyone. That's how I like more popular kids to treat me, instead of ignoring me."

"You've practiced the golden rule. How are things at home?"

I twisted my gold peridot ring from Grandma W. "For a year, I've spent more time with my parents and tried to please. Nothing's enough for them, even going steady with a nice Jewish honor student since last fall. As yearbook editor, Luke won *did most for the school*. Mom promotes a brainy boy who's only a pal over Luke."

"Can you say why?"

"Marcus' blond hair and blue eyes look better with me than Luke's dark coloring. Pretty superficial!" I snickered.

Mr. V smiled. "You feel that parents should model better values than appearance?"

I nodded. "I heard no congratulations from Mom about my valedictorian and other awards."

Mr. V's eyebrows went up in surprise. "You came in first?"

I nodded. "Mom, who got average grades, seems envious. Stuck with her poor opinion of me, I'm lucky to be considered a good person at school and elected class vice president."

"How about your father?"

"They read somewhere that parents must present a united front." I tittered. "Dad goes along with her. Though he perfectionistically criticizes relatives, friends, leaders, you, me, and everyone, he lacks Mom's self-righteous vindictiveness towards me."

"You feel more love from your father?"

"Though things must be done his way, Dad wants me to succeed and be happy." I stole Eva's joke. "My parents need a used daughters' lot to trade me for a better-looking, obedient girl with average brains."

Mr. V chuckled. "Why those traits?"

"Good Jewish boys would keep her too busy to notice gentiles. Wanting to feel smarter than girls they date, most boys choose pretty dumber girls to boost their egos. Virginia Woolf was right: "As long as she thinks of a man, nobody objects to a woman thinking."

"You continue to feel unappreciated at home?"

"And misunderstood...After reading a little cultural anthropology, I agree that education should free people from being automatically stuck in the group of birth! I want outsiders like Negroes and Jews valued for their individual worth, rather than that of the despised groups in which insiders lump them. I feel like a world citizen: free to socialize with anyone and to avoid religious dogma."

"I appreciate hearing your views...do your parents still want more time with you?"

I chuckled. "No. People aren't at their best when criticized. The parents gang up on me less only when Luke's a witness."

Mr. V smiled. "How do you feel about starting college?"

"I'm sad to lose the love and admiration of classmates and teachers. But I can't wait to get away from my parents. Luke's great, but he's going to Rochester. At Barnard, I'll have to work very hard. In my little free time, I'll need lighthearted fun with anyone I like."

"Our time's almost up. Do you want another session?"

"You've been kind to listen and try to get my parents to improve. Despite my satisfying all their demands, they have yet to budge or treat me better. But they could be worse. The parents of a brilliant friend consider college a waste of money for girls. Though Eva would make an exceptional lawyer, her parents expect her to work and pay rent. I'm grateful for my parents' support of my going away to college."

"Congratulations on your honors! If I don't see you, best of luck in college!"

"Thank you very much, Mr. V. I appreciate all your help!"

Friday, July 6, 1962: Reunion

Will last night's intriguing dream come true? Ten years from now, I'm visiting Albany from some far-off city where I live to attend our AHS reunion. It's unclear whether I have a boyfriend or husband. My parents are no longer in Albany. Driving me from my motel to the dinner dance, Craig says, "You look pretty in that blue-and-white halter dress!"

"I appreciate the compliment, Craig! You look handsome, more athletic and muscular!"

"Thank you! Ballet's been marvelous! Dancing for hours every week and lifting female partners have made me stronger. I love touring with our local company when I can get away from my attorney job."

"I'm impressed that a part-time dancer is good enough to make the company and tour in the corps!"

He joked, "They're hard up for males to partner females. Flexibility has helped compensate for starting ballet so late."

I admired his making the world better after hearing, "I feel good as a lawyer working for a non-profit for under-privileged kids." Later, I was in heaven dancing with Craig and feeling his new strength!

Despite looking trimmer and more handsome, electrical engineer Jake still expressed the humble sense of humor we all loved. His younger bride, dressed in a prim navy outfit, had graduated from Albany Catholic girls' schools: Academy of Holy Names and St. Rose College. When Jake and I danced, his wife seemed to frown at me.

Asking about adventurous Dominic, I heard, "In the Navy, he's at sea in the Mediterranean." I wondered whether he visited his Greek relatives. The enjoyable dream ended without information about Luke, other friends, and my family.

Saturday, July 7, 1962: Mixed Feelings

On my half birthday, I'm feeling more emotional than normal with tears flowing. I'll be glad to escape from hypercritical controlling parents, dreadful winter weather, and the corrupt Albany political machine. Reluctant to leave sweet parakeet Tumba, Luke, Doreen, Eva, and other warm appreciative people, I'll miss belonging at school, approval from teachers, and socializing with friends. I'll be sorry to leave my room with ballerina wallpaper, princess phone, satiny desk, and Sara's white dressing table. For two more months, I'll treasure freedom from schoolwork, summer weather, Thacher Park, Rensselaerville, the Boulevard, Mike's Log Cabin, and Stewart's and Toll Gate ice cream! I miss Sara and hope to get up the nerve to call her in NYC.

CHARACTERS

Mom's Family

1875: Grandpa Cline born near Vilna, Lithuania; died 1946

1880: Grandma C born near Minsk, Belarus; died 1960

1898: marriage

1900: immigration to NYC & Gloversville, NY

1903: Uncle Abner born

    Married Rosa

        1932: Beth born Gloversville

            1953: marriage

            1955: June born Long Island, NY

            1957: widowed, remarried in Albany

            1958: Jill born Albany

            1960: Dan born Albany

    Divorce

    1944: married Myrna in Gloversville

        1946: Lydia born

        1949: Ella born

1905: Uncle Peter born

    Married Faith in Gloversville

        1927: Nick born

            1953: marriage

            1954: son born

            1956: son born

            1960: daughter born

1907: Uncle Isaac born; died 1946

1912: Mom Fern born Gloversville
    1937: married Herm in Albany
        1940: Rowena born & died Northville
        1945: I was born Albany
        7/3/54: parakeet Tumba arrived
1917: Aunt Sara born Gloversville
    1940: married George in Albany; divorce 1947
    1948: married Jules in Spring Valley, NY; divorce 1951
    1955-1959: loved Mort, NYC boyfriend

Dad's Family

1876: Grandpa Weiss born The Ukraine; died 1946

1878: Grandma W born The Ukraine; died 1954

1898: marriage

1900: immigration to NYC

1901: Aunt Hannah born NYC

    Married Cal in NYC

        1928: Justine born NYC

            1950: married in NYC

            1953: son Herb born NYC

            1958: daughter Angelina born NYC

1903: Aunt Rhoda born NYC

    1933: married Harvey in NYC

1908: Aunt Lila born NYC

    1933: married Bert in NYC

        1938: Hal born NYC

        1945: Ron born NYC

1911: Dad Herm born NYC

    1937: married Fern in Albany, NY

        1940: Rowena born and died Northville, NY

        1945: I was born Albany

Males in My Life

Name	First Mentioned	Description
Adam	6/10/62	Second cousin
Artie	2/2/57	Past heartthrob
Barry	7/18/60	Asbury Park NJ busboy
Bob	3/23/61	Schoolmate
Craig	9/17/58	Close friend & class leader
Dominic	9/29/59	Crush & close friend
Donald	7/20/58	Catskill romance & pen pal
Eddie	7/18/60	Asbury Park bellhop & date
Frankie	1/1/57	Rabbi's son
Gordon	4/18/60	Eva's date
Hank	9/13/58	Intelligent crush & friend
Herb	8/1/60	Frat dance date
Jake	6/14/60	Crush & close friend
Jay	10/19/61	Eva's date Stanley
Jed	8/26/60	Occasional date
Jerry	2/21/61	Date
Jim	2/14/61	Younger AHS leader & flirt
John	6/22/61	Eva's boyfriend
JP	12/13/59	Doreen's boyfriend
Karl	7/15/54	Dad's friend
Keith	5/5/62	Eva's 1962 boyfriend
Latin class triumvirate	1/2/61	Craig, Dominic, & Jake

Lee	6/16/60	Crush & classmate
Len	4/17/60	Cousin Lydia's boyfriend
Logan	10/3/61	Doreen's RPI boyfriend
Lon	10/13/58	Crush & friend
Luke	9/3/58	Crush & date
Marcus	2/3/56	Brainy classmate & date
Mitch	5/18/57	Past boyfriend
Myles	1/6/57	Past sexy date
Neal	10/26/57	Doreen's crush
Mr. B	8/7/61	Reading teacher
Mr. O	2/19/60	Teacher: debate & yearbook
Mr. P	9/3/58	Hackett teacher
Mr. R	8/7/61	Reading teacher
Mr. V	3/15/61	Social worker
Parker	10/5/59	Godlike senior
Paul	11/9/53	Fascinating ex-boyfriend
Pete	7/21/60	Colombian date
Phil	5/6/59	Date & classmate
Rafi	7/20/60	Asbury Park Israeli date
Ray	11/3/57	Past boyfriend
Rex	2/7/59	Dance partner & nephew of Kirk Douglas
Richie	7/17/60	Asbury Park date
Ric	3/1/60	Eva's 1959 date & crush
Sal	10/31/58	Past infatuation
Stanley	10/19/61	Nickname of Eva's date Jay
Steve	9/9/58	Past boyfriend

Tad	3/12/50	Classmate & husband
Tom	7/4/61	Cousin Lydia's crush
Tony	12/14/60	Eva's 1960-1961 boyfriend
Tumba	7/3/54	My pet parakeet
Ty	2/16/58	Doreen's 1961 prom date
Udeh	1/6/57	Class leader & friend
Victor	12/11/59	Date
Xavier	10/1/59	Eva's classmate
Yeats	10/26/59	Boyfriend
Zeke	11/9/59	Intriguing crush

Females in My Life

Name	First Mentioned	Description
Alice	12/26/60	Former Hackett classmate
Anita	7/19/60	Asbury Park NJ teen guest
Anna	5/21/54	Past Hudson classmate
Bea	7/24/55	Friend since fifth grade
Betty	6/17/60	Classmate
Cara	6/17/60	Classmate & friend
Darlene	4/18/61	Colonie past classmate
Dora	7/5/60	First boss & Mom's friend
Doreen	9/28/54	Close friend since fifth grade
Eileen	1/6/62	Cousin Hal's bride
Eva	12/13/58	Close friend at Schuyler
Evelyn	4/16/57	Mom's friend, Karl's wife
Henrietta	5/30/61	Class secretary & friend
Irene	5/29/57	Classmate since fifth grade
Jennie	11/27/61	Ric's crush
Joan	12/25/60	Cousin Lydia's wild friend
Julia	10/29/55	Friend & party giver
Marie	11/1/58	Classmate
Marsha	10/13/54	Good friend
May	12/14/60	Eva's dramatics group friend
Mista	12/5/61	Exchange student
Robin	4/16/57	Daughter of Karl & Evelyn
Stella	10/19/61	Eva's nickname
Tara	10/14/51	Close friend since first grade

ACKNOWLEDGEMENTS AND PERMISSIONS

Boy Crazy 1960-1962: The High School Diary is a work of historical fiction, which grew out of the author's teen diary. Though the photos are of real people, the actions, dialogue, and qualities of the characters are creations of the author's imagination.

The author is grateful to friends and cousins who provided inspiration for the characters and/or approved the use of photos and memories, such as Eva, Doreen, Ric, Alice, Yeats, Lydia, Hal, Julia, Henrietta, and Udeh.

The author sincerely appreciates the prompt permission granted by Gregg Tallman, Publisher/Owner of *Spotlight Magazine*, to use the print magazine photo under July 19, 1960.

The author thanks Mike Spain, Associate Editor, *Times Union*, for prompt permission to reproduce the newspaper photos under December 14, 1960 (attributed to Sheehan); January 27, 1962; and June 26, 1962.

The author is grateful to Mary Darcy, Executive Producer, *All Over Albany*, for generous permission to use the June 16, 2010, photo from the wonderful online magazine article *The Boulevard Cafeteria: Ticket to Lunch* under February 27, 1960.

Many of the book's photos are from the Albany High School and Schuyler High School yearbooks. The Director of Communication of the Albany Public Schools consulted their attorney, who confirmed that group and individual class and yearbook photos are in the public domain and thus may be used in this book.

The deceased relatives who inspired the characters Aunt Rhoda and Uncle Harvey kindly gave the author the diary, which the author photographed for the book cover. The author, beneficiary of deceased relatives who took various snapshots, is the copyright holder of most of the other photographs, including the dance photo on the front cover.

All efforts have been unsuccessful in identifying current copyright holders of photos for which family members paid, such as the Colman Kuharik wedding photo under June 10, 1962. The original photographers are likely deceased because of the age of the photos. The author's written attempts to contact descendants of deceased photographer Ted Proskin to identify the current copyright holder of the photo under December 9, 1961, went unanswered. Under March 20, 1960, Sara's 1945 photo lacks any photographer name.

The author has been unable to identify the composer and version of *Christmas Bride* lyrics briefly quoted.

The author thanks the Mensa Writers' Group and other writing colleagues for invaluable feedback, which helped improve the book. Special appreciation goes to Alan, Will, Ken, Milt, Susan, Joan, and Greg.

The author very much appreciates cover design assistance and feedback from Kevin, Sherre, Ken, Christine, Bobby, Paula, Jan, Sierra, Will, Carol, Ginny, Tony, Milt, Linda, Alan, and Susan!

Last and far from least, the author is exceptionally thankful for generous, talented Bela's encouragement, appreciation of the book, specific feedback, professional marketing contributions, and invaluable editing and proofreading! He has continued to be outstanding as the masculine incarnation of Clio, the Muse!

AUTHOR BIOGRAPHY

AHS graduation photo

Using her master's degree in psychology, Angela Weiss has enjoyed five diverse careers, including staff writer/graphic artist of in-house books, instructional manuals, research study reports, web pages, and promotional materials. She has ghostwritten biographies and edited books and articles. *Boy Crazy 1960-1962: The High School Diary*, based on her teen journals, is the sequel to *Boy Crazy: The Secret Life of a 1950s Girl*. Still a bit boy crazy, Angela appreciates life in Los Angeles where she enjoys intellectual, cultural, outdoor, and athletic pursuits, especially dancing.

www.ingramcontent.com/pod-product-compliance
Lightning Source LLC
Chambersburg PA
CBHW071448110726
47908CB00003B/550